Tim Ross has moved a lot in his fourteen years. As he is about to enter ninth grade, Tim must move again, this time to Saratoga Springs, New York. The house his parents have rented, sight unseen, is the former home of Victorian author Charles Chatsworth. Chatsworth Mansion turns out to be a monstrosity, right out of a horror movie, with a reputation to match. Most townsfolk think it's haunted.

From bitter experience, Tim knows it's tough to be the new kid in town. But now, added to his usual burdens of being short, brainy, and unfamiliar with local customs, Tim is "a freak living in a freak house."

Bored and lonely, Tim becomes obsessed with finding the key to the mansion's attic. He doesn't know what he will find up there, but he feels certain it will make his life more exciting. He is right.

The Spirit of Chatsworth Mansion

By Alice Scovell Coleman

tiara books

Acknowledgments

Since they have been done out of a dedication, I'll use this page to thank my husband, Stuart, and my three children, Emma, Teddy and Libby, for their unwavering support and enthusiasm. A special shout-out to Libby for reading this book each night as it was being written. Either she really enjoyed it or she liked holding pages warm from the printer.

I also want to thank the very exclusive club of my pre-publication readers who all met the membership requirements of extraordinary intelligence and a willingness to spot typos: Mel Scovell, Roxana Stix Brunell, Diane Darst, Sarah Kagan, Chris Renino, and Susan Berger. Junior club members, Johnny LaZebnik and Nikita Lamba, were especially helpful as representatives of the book's target audience. Let's hope they have a large constituency.

Many thanks to the people of Saratoga Springs, especially the Dunhams and the Arnolds, who welcomed Libby and me to their wonderful town for four summers. We still dream of Putnam Market's blueberry muffins and Mrs. London's brownies!

Three cheers for Anjalé Perrault for juggling her baby, her career, her husband, her dogs, and her house while designing my dream cover at breakneck speed. A cheer also for Alex Isley for lending his discerning eye to artistic matters.

And finally, deep and abiding thanks to my darling mother, Cynthia Scovell, who was not here to read this book. During my childhood, her sprightly nightly reading-aloud made me love reading books which led to my wanting to write them.

For information regarding permission, write to:
Tiara Books
62 Birchall Drive
Scarsdale, NY 10583

ISBN 978-0-972984-61-4
Library of Congress Control No. 2006909127
Coleman, Alice Scovell
The Spirit of Chatsworth Mansion/by Alice Scovell Coleman

Cover illustration by Anjalé Armand Perrault   Text set in Georgia 11.5

PRINTED IN THE UNITED STATES OF AMERICA

To my brilliant siblings...
if I listed all your outstanding
qualities I'd fill this entire book,
so you just get one apiece:

Julie, for her beauty,
Nell, for her wit,
Ted, for his integrity,
And Claire, for her goodness.

With much love, Avis

Chapter One

It was moving day. Most people think moving day is really exciting. It means going to a new place to meet new people and have new experiences. Or they think moving day is really depressing. It means leaving old haunts, saying goodbye to old friends, and being left with old memories. But for me, moving day didn't involve either excitement or sadness. It was just moving day...again.

For the past three years, my parents and I had been living in Scarsdale, New York while I attended middle school. Three years was pretty much a record for my family staying in one place, but I still hadn't managed to parlay the time into any real friendships. I just didn't fit in. On the first day of school, I had made the major mistake of wearing a cowboy hat and boots, standard attire in my old school in Billings, Montana. Standard attire for the Scarsdale crowd was polo shirts, khakis, and topsiders. On my first day in Montana, I had made the major mistake of *not* wearing a cowboy hat and boots, but I didn't know that because I had come from Del Mar, California where everyone wore t-shirts and drawstring shorts.

Still, the Scarsdale cowboy fiasco could have been surmounted, if I had tried hard. I just didn't want to bother. I'm the kind of kid who uses words like "parlayed" and "surmounted," and it's tough to find other kids who'll accept that. And even if I did find those kids, what was the point? I knew that as soon as I found them, my dad and mom would call a "family meeting"—not exactly hard to schedule for the three of us—to announce that they wanted to move.

1

The conversation always went something like this:

Dad (clearing his throat and looking hopeful): Timmy, your mother and I would like to pull up stakes and head... (here, he'd fill in the blank: east, west, north, south).

Mom (jumping in, looking expectant): There's such a great new opportunity for Dad, and we could all use a bit of...(here, she'd fill in the blank: warm weather, clean air, city bustle, country calm).

Dad: But we don't want to do anything unless it's ok with you. No new opportunity, no new environment means enough to us to make our number one son unhappy. So, if you don't want to go, say the word and those stakes stay put.

On more than one occasion, I'd wanted to call their bluff. To say, "I'd like to stay here," but I'd never had the guts to do it. If they agreed to stay, I might settle in, but I might not. Without any guarantees, I couldn't bear to kill their expectant, hopeful looks. It was easier to get out the boxes and suitcases and hit the road again.

All this moving from place to place is because my dad is a journalist. But not one of those journalists who wins the Pulitzer Prize and has his own column in *The New York Times*. My dad specializes in small town newspapers where he covers the local "big" stories, like parking regulations and the school budget. He's always getting offered positions at far-flung papers, for slightly more pay, which he accepts because he enjoys living in different places. It gives him fodder for his real life's work: novel writing. My dad hopes to write the great American novel. Maybe that's why he wants to be personally acquainted with so much of America.

My mom has always been game for a change of scenery, too. Wherever we've moved, she's gotten herself a gig teaching Victorian novels at a local college, but she doesn't care about becoming a professor. She cares about writing articles for scholarly journals on subjects like "The Symbolism of Name Choice in the Works of George Eliot." When I read the titles aloud, I feel like I have dry cotton-balls in my mouth. My mom really loves that stuff, and she cries with happiness when some minor journal, which nobody ever reads, accepts her piece. When a journal rejects her work, my mom doesn't cry, but she puts herself to bed, whatever the time of day, and tells me to fend for myself. Not that, even on a good day, she's the nurturing, maternal type. Don't get me wrong, I'm not abused or even neglected. My parents love me wholeheartedly in their own, weird way. It's just that neither of my parents is very domestic. They don't fret over interior decorating, preferring to rent fully furnished quarters. And they don't fuss over cooking, preferring to eat take-out food, with a focus on regional delicacies. In California, we ate lots of tacos and salads; in Montana, tons of steaks and burgers; and in Scarsdale, loads of blintzes and bagels. Of course, diverse fare is available in all those places, even in Montana, but my parents always focus on the "foods of the friendly natives." Maybe we keep moving because, eventually, my parents get sick of their regional diets. Fortunately, wherever we live, I'm allowed to eat pizza. I've eaten a lot of pizza in my day.

Two days ago, I'd learned that we'd be sampling new foods from a new place. I'd had an inkling that a move was in the air. The tell-tale signs had all been evident: the purchase of bubble wrap and masking tape, a purge of old clothes from the closets, a dwindling of staples in the refrigerator, and a trip to the local garage for a tune-up.

My parents had called a family meeting in the tiny living room of our tiny apartment near the Scarsdale train station. My dad did his traditional throat clearing and said, "Timmy, early fall always feels like the perfect time of year for a change. We've had a great time here in Scarsdale--you at the Middle School, mom at Sarah Lawrence, and I at *The Scarsdale Inquirer*. But now we have an opportunity for greener pastures, literally and figuratively, in Saratoga Springs, New York."

Like clockwork, Mom chimed in, telling me about Saratoga's beautiful, rural setting. Then she said proudly, "Dad has been invited to be the editor-in-chief of *The Saratogian* which covers local news as well as national and international. Dad has big plans to improve the paper."

Dad said with equal pride, "Mom will be a Lecturer at Skidmore College, teaching Victorian writers, including her beloved Charlotte Bronte, George Eliot, and Charles Dickens."

Next, Mom addressed the advantages for me, pointing out that I would go from being a "little fish in a big pond," by which she referred to all my bright, competitive Scarsdale classmates, to being "a *little* fish in a little pond." Here, my parents chuckled. She should have said, "a *big* fish in a little pond," but she was alluding to my height, or better put, the lack thereof. I had turned fourteen back in June, but I was still the size of many sixth graders. I was convinced that my parents had cursed me by naming me "Tim" after the diminutive Dickens character in *A Christmas Carol.*

After their chuckle, Mom assured me that we still would be living within easy visiting distance of my grandparents—the easy distance had been a key selling-point in the move from Billings to Scarsdale—and that the four would travel from Boston to Saratoga often. She paused, so I had said, with the little enthusiasm I could muster, "Great."

Then she had moved in for the kill. "There's something special we want to tell you about the house we've rented."

"It's a house? That's great." This time my enthusiasm was genuine. I hated the apartment's cramped quarters.

"It's not just any house. It's..." She paused again, like the news was too good to be true, and she and my dad exchanged goofy, ear-to-ear grins. Then she said quickly, "...the house Charles Chatsworth built!"

I had no idea what she was talking about. Was I supposed to know this guy? Not wanting to ruin the grin-fest, I mumbled a noncommittal, "That's nice."

Dad said, "Why, Susan, I believe we've discovered a gap in old Timmy's knowledge. Kind of a relief to find there's still stuff we can teach him." He turned to me, "Charles Chatsworth was a major Victorian writer. In his day, only..." here my Dad made quotation marks with the index and middle fingers of each hand, " 'the other Charles'--Dickens--was as popular. Like Dickens, Chatsworth's novels were sold first as serials and, later, in bound volumes."

I had visions of tour buses filled with ardent fans ringing our doorbell. I hoped that some parents would drag along their beautiful daughters, who would be more interested in a private tour of my room than the group tour of Chatworth's library. Still, I wasn't sure if I had the picture right. "If he was such a great writer, why haven't I ever heard of him?" I asked.

My mother took a turn. "We didn't say he was a *great* writer, we said he was a *popular* one...in his day. For modern readers, his plots depend too heavily on implausible coincidence and his characters aren't vivid like Dickens'. Plus, Chatsworth is wildly wordy. His descriptions go on for pages and pages, and no one has the time for such verbiage. Very few people read him any more, and most of his works have gone out-of-print. However, at the request of the college, I'll be including a Chatsworth novel in my course. The folks of Saratoga still carry the torch for Chatsworth because he, at the height of his glory, chose to live among them."

I have to admit, this whole exchange was starting to irritate me. "So, what, exactly, is the advantage of our living in the house? Is it a mansion?"

"Timmy, I'm surprised at you," said my mother, looking hurt. "I admit that we don't know exactly what the house looks like...we took it sight unseen from a broker once we heard the price. But the advantage is that Chatsworth's spirit will be an inspiration to both your father and me. You know how Dad sometimes gets writer's block? Well, we feel confident that Chatsworth will help him over it. And you know how sometimes I flounder for article ideas? Well, we believe Chatsworth will help guide me."

It took all my control not to roll my eyes. My mother sure had some wacky ideas. Still, I held my tongue. What was the point of arguing? I didn't really want to stay in Scarsdale, with my lack of friends and our cramped quarters, so I played along. I said I hoped that Charles had been good at math because I had to take the New York State Regents and could use some help.

My dad tousled my hair, and said, "Enough with the talking. Let's get to packing."

So, we did. We threw our clothes into suitcases, our books into boxes, linens and towels into garbage bags, and carefully wrapped our three computers in bubble wrap and tape. We had no furniture or even television to move, just a few knick-knacks, lamps, my bicycle, and some photos.

Before I packed my computer, though, I did a quick Goggle search on Chatsworth. It didn't turn up much information besides his lifespan and the titles of his novels. Like my mom said, Chatsworth had been immensely popular in his day, but had fallen into obscurity soon after his death. Sort of the reverse of Vincent van Gogh who sold only one painting during his life, but whose paintings now sold for tens of millions of dollars. I had written a paper on van Gogh for my eighth grade history class, and it seemed tragic that he died thinking himself an utter failure. I wondered which would be better: to have your work admired during your life and scorned after your death, or the reverse?

With so much to get done, though, I didn't have time to ponder the question. We barely managed to clean up the apartment before we had to load our belongings into our old red station wagon to start the three hour trip to Saratoga Springs and the house that Charles built.

Chapter Two

By the time we saw the Northway sign listing the three Saratoga Springs exits, we were running late for our appointment with the realtor. Both my parents hate to be late for anything. To make matters worse, my mom couldn't tell from the map which exit was ours.

Without saying a word, I passed forward the directions from Scarsdale to Skidmore which I had printed out from Mapquest before packing my computer. I had been on too many trips with my parents to rely on their navigational skills. And I never relied on their skills with any modern technology. My parents seemed to secretly wish they were living in Victorian times. If they could have, my parents would have ridden to Saratoga in a horse-drawn carriage. That would have kept the realtor waiting a really long time.

"Thank you, dear," my mother said as she took the directions. She smiled back at me, crammed in the corner of the backseat with lamps at my feet and big plastic bags of linens threatening my death by suffocation. She looked at the print-out and, just in time, read aloud, "We take exit 14 and at the end of the ramp, turn right."

My dad swerved, making the tires squeal and the car behind us honk, but we made it. The two peanut butter and jelly sandwiches I had eaten half an hour before sloshed in my stomach. I cracked opened my window to get some air. It smelled fresh and clean.

The road off the highway soon became a tree-lined avenue with a speed limit of twenty-five. In the early September sunlight, the overhead canopy of lush leaves glowed green. After about a mile, on the left, we saw the entrance gate for the famous Saratoga Springs Racetrack, and a little farther on the right there was a shack-like pizzeria you couldn't miss, because it was painted blue, named Bruno's. I could now relax: in Saratoga, I wouldn't starve.

After a few twists and turns, we made a right on main street, which in Saratoga is called "Broadway." Not exactly like its namesake in Manhattan, with its flashing lights, crowd-choked sidewalks, and blaring horns. This Broadway was dominated by a brown and yellow Victorian hotel, The Adelphi, which had three-story-high slender columns and elaborate fretwork. Although over a century old, the building looked brand new. If it hadn't been for a few national chain stores--Starbucks, The Gap, and Borders--I would have believed that I had stepped back in time.

Since my Mapquest directions weren't to the house, we had to pull over to ask for help. Dad eased the station wagon into a parking space in front of Wheat Fields Restaurant and told me to find a "likely candidate." I got out of the car, stretched my legs and, through the windshield, gave my parents a thumbs-up. My dad dramatically pointed with his right hand to the watch on his left wrist.

I wanted to hurry, but the first person coming toward me was a hippie guy with long blond hair, accented with blue streaks. This town seemed to have a thing for the color blue. There was no way this cool guy would want to be seen talking to a kid in a polo shirt and khakis, so I let him pass. Then a little kid, maybe about four years old, and his mother approached. She looked nice enough, but the kid was wailing that he wanted to go to the toy store across the street. I let them walk by. Or rather, the mother walked, the kid was dragged. Then--bingo!--along came a well-dressed elderly man with white hair and a kindly-look.

"Excuse me, sir," I said, "I'm from out of town, and I need some directions. Do you think you could help me?"

"Well, I won't know until I try. What are you looking for?" he asked.

"I'm looking for the Chatsworth house."

"You mean, Chatsworth Mansion?"

I couldn't believe that my parents could afford a place that had "mansion" is its title. "I'm not sure if it's the same place. I'm looking for the house where the writer Charles Chatsworth lived."

"That would be Chatsworth Mansion."

We were moving up in the world. From cramped apartment to Victorian mansion. At this rate, our next move would be to the Taj Mahal.

I said, "Great. Then, can you tell me how to get there?" Out of the corner of my eye, I could see my dad vigorously doing the watch-pointing thing again.

"Are you a rare fan of Chatsworth's writing, seeking to pay homage? Because if you are, I'm sorry to say that there's no special plaque or marker. You would do better to go to the cemetery to visit his grave. He has a pretty snazzy monument."

"Oh, it's nothing like that. My parents and I," here, I gestured with my hand toward our packed car, "are going to live in Chatsworth House. I mean, Mansion."

The old man looked startled and asked, his voice heavy with disbelief, "You're going to live there?"

"That's the plan."

"Is it really?" His eyebrows were knit in concern.

"Unless you tell me a reason not to."

The old man gave himself a little shake and his face relaxed into a smile. He said, "Where are my manners? Welcome to Saratoga Springs." He put out his hand and I shook it. "I'm Amos Henry, and we'll be neighbors. I live just a few houses away, in a smaller Victorian, painted yellow with white trim. Sorry if I seemed surprised at your news. It's just that Chatsworth Mansion has been empty for quite a spell." He noticed, through the windshield, that my dad's

9

face was turning red. "But I've kept you chatting long enough. You need directions. Continue straight along this road and in, about half a mile or so, you'll see, on this side, a dark gray house with white trim, up on a hill. You can't miss it."

"Thanks," I said. "It's very nice to meet you."

"Nice to meet you, too, ahh...." He paused, and I realized I hadn't supplied my name.

"Tim. Tim Ross."

"I'll see you around, I'm sure. Saratoga isn't very big." he said.

"Bye," I said, and I started to walk back to the car.

"Tim," he called before I opened the door. I turned back to look at him. "I wish you good luck."

Maybe I was being hyper-sensitive, but I swear he said it as if he thought I needed it.

* * *

By the time we pulled up to the house, at the top of the long, steep driveway, we were eighteen minutes late. Not such a terrible delay given the two hundred miles we had traveled. As soon as my dad parked our Volvo next to the big black Mercedes in the front, he jumped out of the car to meet the realtor, a Mrs. Ellen Stilton, who was talking into her cell phone and tapping her foot. She was a petite woman in her late forties, very thin, with shoulder-length streaked blonde hair, and a heavily painted, angular face.

She said loudly into the phone, "I gotta go. They're *finally* here." Then she snapped the lid shut.

My dad held out his hand, which she limply shook. "Mrs. Stilton, I'm David Ross." Mom and I approached them. "And this is my wife, Susan, and our son, Timmy."

Mrs. Stilton did not extend her hand for shaking. My dad continued, "We apologize for being a little late. We had to pack and travel today."

Most people, especially if they're expecting checks to change hands, would have said, "No need to apologize. As

10

you can see, I worked while I waited." But Mrs. Stilton wasn't most people. All she said, irritably, was, "Because you're late, we'll have to hurry. I have another appointment this afternoon, Mr. Ross."

"Please call me, David," said my dad, loath to alienate any Saratogians on the very first day.

Most people would have said, "Of course, and you can call me Ellen," but Mrs. Stilton said no such thing. All she said was, "Did you bring the checks?"

"Yes," said my mom, sounding a bit irritated herself. "But before we tender them, we need to see the house."

This assertion, with its subtle threat, sounded pretty hollow. Unless the inside of the house was rotten with cobwebs, spiders, beetles, dust, and mice like the infamous Miss Havisham's, we were staying. We had never lived in such grand style, even in Montana. As we had driven up the driveway, my dad had marveled that the rent for the mansion was less than for the tiny Scarsdale apartment. By my calculation, you could fit about fifteen of the apartments into this one house.

And the house wasn't just spacious, it was imposing. Especially when you looked up at its gray eminence, surrounded by ancient trees, from down below on the street. It had a turret, as well as a main back section and a smaller front section, each with lots of architectural details and its own mansard roof. A mansard roof is flat on top with four curved, sloping sides, like the roofs in *Psycho* or *The Addams Family*. Unfortunately, it wasn't just the roof, but the entire house, that looked like it belonged in a horror movie. Being painted dark gray didn't help, and neither did being isolated from all the cheerful houses on the street.

Still, the house was going to be our home if the inside was anything above condemnable. Which it definitely was. Once we entered, we saw that the house had been well preserved. The air was a bit musty, but nothing that opening some windows couldn't fix. Mrs. Stilton swept through the foyer,

11

her high heels clattering across the wooden floors, and we struggled to keep up with her. She mentioned to my parents that the out-of-town owners were interested in selling, but having gotten a load of our beat-up old car, she clearly had ruled us out as potential buyers. My dad asked the price and expressed interest. It was so reasonable, cheap even, but I didn't think my parents could afford a house. They certainly had never expressed a desire to buy one. It's tough to move on two days' notice if you have to sell. I assumed my dad was just playing along with Mrs. Stilton to thaw out her you-kept-me-waiting iciness.

As Mrs. Stilton tore through the first and second floors, instead of pointing out the incredible architectural details, of which there were many, she focused on all the things we wouldn't need, like the closet space, the modern kitchen appliances, and the cable TV line. I was happy to hear that the house had been partially wired for computers, that the big claw-footed bathtub on the second floor worked, and that the high school bus stopped just a few houses down the street. Actually, Mrs. Stilton had first told me that the *middle* school bus stopped around the corner, but my mother, all indignant, had jumped in.

"Timothy isn't going to the *middle* school. Timothy is going to the *high* school." Suddenly, I wasn't "Tiny Tim" or "Timmy" or even "Tim;" I was "Timothy." In fairness to Mrs. Stilton, Sherlock Holmes would have made the same mistake.

Upon hearing the news, Mrs. Stilton got all animated and asked me, "What grade are you going into?"

"Ninth."

"Like my Stephanie! I'm sure that, by the end of the first day, you'll know who Stephanie Stilton is." She turned to my mom, "Single-handedly, she ran the middle school. She was the president of the student council, the head cheerleader, and captain of the soccer team. If she stays on the same

12

path, we'll all be voting for her as President of the US of A in no time."

"She won't have my vote. I'll be voting for Timmy in that election," grumbled my dad. I guess he had decided that it wouldn't be so bad to alienate a person in Saratoga, as long as it was this one.

Mrs. Stilton didn't look pleased, but she chose to laugh. "Well, as long as she has Tommy's vote for ninth grade rep, we won't worry about your vote. Will we?" she asked me, conspiratorially.

I had heard her call me "Tommy," but, being averse to confrontation, I let it go. I was certain that, even if I corrected her, she would repeat the mistake five minutes later. Maybe it would be easier to concede the point and change my birth certificate.

Mrs. Stilton had arrived at yet another linen closet, threw open the doors, and let out a satisfied sigh.

All along, Mrs. Stilton had been flinging open every closed door, but when we got to a closed door on the third floor, she hurried by it. As I passed the door, I tried turning the handle and found it was locked.

"Where does this door lead to?" I called out to Mrs. Stilton, who was forced to stop and turn around. From the rigors of dashing about the hot house, she was sweating pretty heavily, causing her make-up to run. She looked like a creature from a house of horrors.

"To the attic," she answered, disdainfully. Her good humor toward a potential vote for darling Stephanie seemed to have evaporated in the thick, hot air of the third floor.

"Then why is it locked?" I asked.

"I really couldn't say. Maybe there are bats up there."

"Bats?!" shouted my mom, turning pale. She turned to my dad, "If there are bats, I think we should reconsider...."

Both my dad and I knew exactly what was going on. My mother, who lives her life immersed in Victoriana, has an irrational fear of diseases that were fatal in the nineteenth century. She doesn't get that many of those diseases now have treatments or cures. So when someone she knows gets pneumonia, or she reads about a case of tuberculosis or rabies, she gets crazy with worry. Bats are notorious carriers of rabies.

Mrs. Stilton didn't get what was happening, but she was shrewd enough to see that the transaction was in jeopardy. She back-pedaled fast. "I didn't say there *are* bats up there. In fact, I'm sure there aren't. The door is probably locked because it locks automatically."

"Do you have the key to open it?" I was being pushy, but I've always wanted to poke around an old attic. When visiting my grandparents, I'd seen some Antiques Roadshow episodes where people brought in valuable treasures they had unearthed in their attics, and I was ready for my share of a windfall.

"I just have the front door key and the back door key, but I'm sure, Tommy, that a curious boy like you will find it."

She made a point of consulting her diamond-studded gold watch. "Well, I really must run. *Some* people show up on time for their appointments, and I hate to keep them waiting. I have a few papers downstairs for you to sign and, of course, I can't leave without the two checks. Shall we?" She pointed to the stairs and we all followed her down to the first floor.

Chapter Three

As soon as she was gone, we looked at each other and laughed. My dad said, "Hey, *President Tommy*, do you think you could take a break from running the country to help your mother open some windows? I'm going to start carrying in the boxes. They've been in the car for so long, and I hate to keep them waiting."

I was glad to stay inside, even if the heat was stifling. I wanted a chance to look around on my own.

Once my father left, my mother asked, "What do you think, Timmy? Do you like it?"

"It's nice, Mom, but I'm not sure it's big enough. We may have to add another floor or two."

She laughed. "Do you realize that there are enough bedrooms on the second floor for you to sleep in a different one every night of the week? Not that I recommend it. You should probably choose one."

"I think I'll go for the round room." That was the bedroom in the turret. It wasn't the biggest room, but it was the coolest. Plus, it was on the other side of the floor from the master bedroom, which at my age seemed like a good choice.

"I was hoping you'd say that. If you take the round room, you can play your indoor basketball thing whenever you want to without disturbing us."

My "indoor basket ball thing" was a hoop on a backboard that hooked over the top of any door. The hoop came with a lightweight foam ball for shooting. Wherever we've lived, my bedroom has become official when I've hung up my hoop. Then, whenever I'm bored or unhappy, playing a little one-on-none makes me feel better. The problem is, my parents don't appreciate the constant banging or my sports announcer commentary. In the Scarsdale apartment, my indoor basketball games had become a bone of contention.

"With all the practice I'll get, I'll be ready to go pro. Just you wait, Mom, I'll be bringing in the big basketball bucks, and then I'll set you up in a huge Victorian mansion."

My mom laughed again. "You know, I had a good feeling about this house when we first heard about it. I wasn't so sure when we got here, but now that the Stilton woman is gone, the good feeling has come back. I just know great things are going to happen to us here." She gave me a hug. "We'd better get to work. How about I take the upstairs and you take this floor?"

* * *

Going from room to room to open windows gave me a chance to see Chatsworth Mansion at a more reasonable pace. My assignment was hard work since about half the windows were stuck--either warped with age or painted in-- but I liked looking at the rooms and felt secretly triumphant every time I pried a window open.

I was already pretty familiar with Victorian homes, having been dragged to many of them in England. My parents were hell-bent on seeing all the places that their favorite authors had lived in. Over the years, I had grudgingly learned a lot about Victorian design and could describe its features with the best of them. However, I had never been in a more de-tailed example of Victorian style than Chatsworth Mansion. Every room was a variation on the theme of wood, wood, and more wood. Actually, I should have said "woods" because each room had plenty of tiger maple, with its golden glow, and mahogany, with its rich redness. I had never seen wood so lavishly incorporated into a house; it was everywhere, from wainscoting to paneling to carved door and window frames, to massive mantel pieces, to coffered ceilings. No

16

detail had been overlooked, no expense had been spared. Although the ornate decoration was not exactly appealing to a modern eye, especially mine which was used to folding chairs and cement-block bookcases, it was impressive.

When I reached the library, having already opened windows in the living room and dining room, I paused to look at the massive mahogany desk in the center. The desk must have been Charles Chatsworth's, since its Victorian grandeur fit the surroundings perfectly. Measuring about nine feet by eight feet, the desk was heavily carved, with four inset panels of urns with flowers bordered by four figural columns of women. It had to be worth a fortune; that is, if it could ever be moved. It must have been assembled on the spot, because, between its weight and size, it could never leave the room. If my dad set up his novel-writing operations on this desk, he would definitely be inspired.

Dad couldn't try out the desk yet, though, because there was no chair. It suddenly occurred to me that the attic might hold some stray Victorian furniture. Not priceless pieces, of course, but maybe a few end tables and small chairs. They would come in handy, to fill out the sparse modern furnishings. But how to get the attic door unlocked? My parents wouldn't allow me to break in and they wouldn't pay for a locksmith. After all, even without the attic, we had more space than we could use. Since I wanted a chance to explore the attic on my own, I decided not to say anything to my parents. I would just have to find the key.

I eyed the desk more critically and my heart started beating faster. Maybe somebody, maybe even Charles Chatsworth himself, had hidden the attic key in the desk. If the key was there, I was the person to find it. Unbeknownst to Ellen Stilton, I really was a "curious boy" who could find things. I had cut my teeth on Encyclopedia Brown at the age of six and, at eight, had moved on to Sherlock Holmes. I had whipped through the works of Agatha Christie, Dashiell Hammett, Dorothy Sayers and a slew of other detective writers. From the experts, I had learned many tricks of the trade.

Unfortunately, my powers of observation and deduction were rarely needed. My last case was in second grade, when I was living in Del Mar. On that fateful day, the school's fund-raising "guess-how-many" jar, filled with Hershey's kisses, was suddenly half empty. Just as I had started questioning my classmates, Billy Bates complained to the teacher that his stomach hurt and that he wanted to go home early. He opened his locker to get his jacket, and several silver wrappers fluttered out. Case closed.

My other detective opportunities were not hands-on. Wherever we lived, if the police were stumped on a case, my dad would give me the details, and we would talk through the possible solutions. But mysteries are rare in small towns, and my life had not been very exciting. I hoped the key would change all that.

I started my search of the desk by checking all around its outside. I pressed on the panels, looked carefully for any secret compartments, and ran my fingers over every nook and cranny. Nothing. Then I opened each of the eight huge side drawers. I found a few stray pencils, pens, rubber-bands and paper clips, but no key. I carefully removed each drawer and checked its sides and bottom, in case the key had been taped there. While each drawer was out, I checked the its slot inside the desk. Nothing.

I finally allowed myself to check the most likely hiding place: the narrow middle drawer. I opened it slowly, without looking, wanting to remain hopeful for as long as possible. When it was fully opened, I looked. It was empty. Then I gave the middle drawer and its desk slot the same meticulous scrutiny as the side drawers. No key. I did find, in the back of the slot, three yellowed scraps of paper with old-fashioned handwriting in ink. The papers had written on them *Princess Elizabeth*, *Count Fleet*, and *Emperor of Norfolk* with some numbers across the bottom. They were probably

18

character names and page numbers scribbled by Chatsworth. I put the notes into my pants' pocket for later consideration. Now I knew that I didn't need Chatsworth's spirit to help me with math...I needed it to help me find the key.

* * *

When we had finished opening the windows and unloading the car, my parents began to unpack while I attempted to connect our computers and printer in a household network. While eschewing most modern technology, my parents did accept computers as evil necessities.

At about four o'clock my dad found me in my bedroom, wrestling with some glitches, and said, "Hey, Columbus, why don't you take advantage of the remaining sunlight and discover the new world? Maybe you can find us a good place to eat our first Saratogian supper."

He didn't get any argument from me. After a quick shower and a change of clothes, I rode off on my bicycle. Skidmore was to the right, within walking distance, and town to the left. I went left. A few houses down I spotted a pleasant yellow and white Victorian. Mr. Henry's house. I hadn't noticed it when we first drove by, having been focused on finding our new house. If there was time, I'd stop by later. I had a question to ask Mr. Henry.

The town of Saratoga was even nicer on second viewing. The main street had a good mix of restaurants, clothing stores, book stores, art galleries, florists, and banks. There was a bakery, Mrs. London's, where everything in the case screamed, "Eat me." I answered the call of a thick, moist brownie and was glad I did. I also discovered a take-out store called Putnam Market which had all sorts of tempting prepared foods. I definitely would not starve in Saratoga.

I explored up and down the hilly side streets and saw many more small restaurants, a used book store, a knitting shop, and some hippie clothing stores. There was a large park, with a restored carousel at its edge, but I didn't linger. I found *The Saratogian* headquarters, a small brick building, and near it the town library, which was plain on the outside and amazing on the inside. I guess the long, hard Saratoga winters made readers out of everyone.

Satisfied that I now knew the general lay of the land, I headed back toward home. As I approached Mr. Henry's house, I slowed down. I wanted to visit, but I didn't feel comfortable ringing his doorbell. He hadn't invited me over; he had just said he would see me around. Still, I hoped I might find him outside enjoying the end of a beautiful day.

Chapter Four

Just as I had hoped, I found Mr. Henry sitting on his open Victorian porch, drinking a tall glass of iced tea. He waved to me, and I pulled over.

"Hey, Mr. Henry."

"Hi, Tim. Did you discover the wonders of Saratoga?"

"I did. Especially the brownies at Mrs. London's."

He sighed. "Ah, those are one of the wonders of the world. And the scones are equally spectacular."

I must have been eyeing his iced tea enviously, because he said, "Something about you makes me forget my manners. May I get you something to drink?"

I asked for water; between the brownie, the heat, and the biking, I was awfully thirsty.

"Coming right up," he said. "Make yourself at home." He gestured to a chair, then hurried inside.

I lay my bike down and took a seat. There was a copy of *The Saratogian* on the porch table, which I leafed through. For a small town newspaper, it was pretty impressive.

Mr. Henry emerged and handed me a glass of cold water. I gulped it down.

"Saratoga water is delicious," I said, putting my empty glass on the table.

"Actually, that's Poland Springs," he said. "I'm not a big fan of Saratoga tap water. Too minerally."

"Really? I thought Saratoga was known for its water."

"For its *spring* water, but that's not what comes out of the tap. To drink the spring water, you either have to go to the

21

spring or buy it bottled. If you like bubbly water, I recommend Saratoga Springs Water, in the beautiful blue bottle. Or, if you want an intense water experience, go to the spa and bathe in it. For hundreds of years, people have thought that Saratoga water was a cure for just about everything. It was the water that put Saratoga on the map, and then horseracing kept it there."

"When did people start coming for the water?"

"They started coming in droves in the late 1820s. Many distinguished Victorians came, like Daniel Webster, Edgar Allan Poe, Nathaniel Hawthorne, and James Fenimore Cooper."

"Don't forget Charles Chatsworth."

"That's hard to do when I see his house everyday."

"Which brings us to the question of the day."

"I didn't know there was a question of the day," said Mr. Henry with a smile.

"There is. And it is: what's wrong with Chatsworth Mansion?"

His smile faded. "I'm not sure what you're asking me. If you're asking me whether the faucets leak or the heat is uneven, I have no idea."

"I'm asking you why the rent we're paying for the house is less than for most small apartments here? I just looked at rentals in the paper, and ours is way under market. This morning, you told me that the house has been empty a long time. Why?"

"Well, it does have some issues. Like the driveway is murder in the winter, and it costs a small fortune to heat. And, let's be honest, it's not exactly a pretty house. It's historically interesting, but it's also kind of ugly."

"Mr. Henry, you know there's something more to it. When I said we were going to live there, you looked startled. I wish you'd tell me why."

He sighed. "Ok, Tim, I'll tell you, but it's a long story. Do you have time?"

I checked my watch. We usually ate dinner at about seven. That gave me over an hour. I nodded.

"I know the story of Chatsworth Mansion well because my grandmother, my mother's mother, grew up in Saratoga. She knew firsthand all about Charles Chatsworth, although she was a young girl when he lived here. She used to tell me the story, and I liked it so much that I made her tell it over and over.

"She always started by saying that Charles Chatsworth was world-famous. In the mid-1800's, his works were widely read in both England and the United States. He had fame and fortune, but he also had troubles. He had been married to a woman he adored--her name was Margaret--who he used as the model for all his beautiful ingénues. Their union brought two children, sons. Tragically, when the older boy was in his mid-teens, he died in a boating accident. In those days, especially in England, the first son was the focus of the family, the heir apparent, and Margaret felt the loss keenly. She never recovered from the shock and died within a year's time, just like a Chatsworth heroine would do.

"Chatsworth was wifeless and his remaining son--his name was Edmund--was motherless. Chatsworth vowed to remarry and fast. Unfortunately, he didn't realize that he was an easy mark. When he had married Margaret, he had been a struggling writer; now he was a rich and famous man. He met an actress named Hattie Fields, who had never been successful on stage, but must have been accomplished off-stage, because within a few weeks she had convinced Chatsworth to marry her. Hattie had a son a few years older than Edmund, and Chatsworth rejoiced that he was giving Edmund replacements for both his mother and brother.

"After the marriage, Chatsworth's health took a turn for the worse, maybe from domestic strife or maybe from over-work. Whatever the cause, the 'cure' was to be the waters of Saratoga. Chatsworth had heard from some of his writer friends, some of the very ones I mentioned a few minutes

23

ago, that a trip to Saratoga would restore his health and vigor. Hattie latched onto the idea with enthusiasm. I suppose she didn't like Chatsworth's London friends who saw through her. And, of course, Saratoga was an appealing alternative. It was the height of fashion in the 1870's, especially in the summer, and Hattie liked being part of the social whirl.

"She convinced Chatsworth that they should move to Saratoga permanently, but that they would need a proper place to live. He obliged by having the mansion built in record time, paying hefty premiums to get the work done. All four of them--Chatsworth, Hattie, Edmund and Hattie's son--moved in as soon as it was done."

I interrupted, "What year was that?"

"I'm not sure exactly. Sometime in the late 1870's. Now, where was I? Oh yes, they had just moved in. So, Chatsworth came to Saratoga looking for a cure, but all he got was heartache. Edmund started acting strange, complaining of illness, wandering around town, and escaping frequently to the mansion's roof. He probably was still grieving over his lost mother, and he must have been terribly homesick. Then, one night, he did the unthinkable. As usual, he had gone up to the roof, but this time he threw himself off and fell to his death."

"That's awful," I said. "But that was long ago. The tragedy can't still be scaring people away."

"True, but the tragedy had short-term consequences which begot long-term ones. You see, Chatsworth was inconsolable, blaming himself for his son's death. And in those days, suicide brought shame on the family. I'm not sure whether Edmund was even allowed a proper burial. The loss of Edmund proved too much for the sickly Chatsworth, and he died shortly thereafter.

"At first, Hattie and her son said that they would remain in Saratoga. Certainly, they could afford to, since Chatsworth had left his widow everything, but then one day, without warning, they were gone. Eventually, word spread that they had moved to the Continent, and they were never heard from again. The house was put up for sale, but the tragic events kept buyers away. Years passed until, finally, around the turn of the century, a family moved in.

"They had a lovely little girl named Rose, about my mother's age. While in the house, Rose became strongly attached to an imaginary friend, and her parents played along. But as she got older, Rose grew insistent that her friend wasn't imaginary, that he was a ghost who she could see and hear, and her parents became alarmed. They feared that the child was not right in the head and, loath to commit her to an asylum, they moved away. The town buzzed with the story of the mansion's ghost and, once again, the house stood empty for years.

"Finally, when I was a boy, another family took a chance. I knew their son Peter, but I didn't like him very much. He was the kind of boy who would come over to play, only to steal money from your piggy bank and then deny it. As you can imagine, after he had lived in town for a few months, nobody wanted to play with him. Then he started claiming that there was ghost in his house and, suddenly, everyone wanted to be with him. I assume that he had overheard grown-ups telling the stories, and he seized on the idea for attention.

"In time, though, kids got tired of hearing his stories and wanted to see for themselves. He took a group of them over to the house, up to the attic where he said the ghost lived. The kids were all worked up, trying to seem brave, but feeling terrified. They waited for over an hour--Peter kept saying that the ghost was right there and "repeating" things the ghost said--but nobody saw anything. The whole town heard of the episode. Some parents thought Peter was a bold-faced liar, others thought he was crazy, and still others thought he was wicked for frightening the younger children.

All the parents refused to have their children play with him. To give their son another chance, the family had to move.

"That should have been the end of the ghost rumor, but some skittish people in town continued to believe the house was haunted. From time to time, the house was rented by people needing a lot of space at a bargain price. Some artists lived there and then some beatniks and later some hippies. Then, in the early 80's, the house was bought by a young couple. Have you ever heard of the movie "The Amityville Horror"?"

"I've never seen it," I replied, "But it's about a haunted house, right?"

"Right, and it was supposedly based on a true story. Chatsworth Mansion was another 'true haunted house' and the young owners thought its reputation could be exploited as a business--a bed and breakfast--to satisfy the public's fascination with ghosts. To accentuate the house's eerie appearance, they painted it dark gray. They also upgraded the bathrooms and kitchen. Unfortunately, the business was a dismal failure. Guests who came hoping to see a ghost, went away disappointed. There wasn't anything going bump in the night. And, understandably, no one would come who was truly afraid of ghosts.

"Then a builder wanted to buy the house as a teardown but, to gain tax breaks, the innkeepers had secured a listing with the National Register of Historic Houses. Such houses, can never be torn down; in fact, they can scarcely be altered. The builder backed out.

"Eventually, two science professors at Skidmore, with three young children, bought it. The scientists laughed at the foolish ghost stories, but their children were not as skeptical. They were harassed at school for living in the house, and the youngest, a five year old girl, had trouble sleeping. She became so anxious that, when her parents got an offer to teach in Philly, they took it.

"Which, finally, I'm relieved to say, brings us to the present day."

I didn't know what to think. Part of me wanted the house to be haunted and part of me didn't. "Do you believe the house is haunted?" I asked.

Mr. Henry said firmly, "No I do not. I believe it is only 'the ghost of a ghost' haunting Chatsworth Mansion."

"Then why did you hesitate to tell me?"

"I hate to spread ridiculous rumors. But I suspect you would have heard about it at school sooner or later. I know it's hard to be a new kid, and the house may further complicate matters."

I tried to put on a brave face. "Oh, don't worry about that. I've been the 'new kid' lots of times. I'm sure I can handle it."

Inside, I wasn't so sure. Now, in addition to being short, and bookish, and untutored in local customs, I would be the kid living in the haunted house.

I got up to go home and noticed that, while we were talking, clouds had moved in and, suddenly, the beautiful day was over.

Chapter Five

I was sitting all alone in one of those chairs with a built-in desk arm, waiting for the homeroom bell to ring. On the bus ride to school I had been equally alone. My stop had been the first, so I had had my pick of seats. After moving about half-way to the back--not wanting to be a front-sitting nerd or a back-sitting delinquent--I had slid over to the window seat. At each stop, kids had gotten on and eyed the empty seat next to me, then chosen a different seat. By the end, the bus had been packed, but the seat next to me had remained empty. Not that I had been surprised.

At least it wasn't my clothing that isolated me this time. I had begged my parents for some money and gone to the Gap the day before. A salesgirl with a ring in her nose had helped me to pick out appropriate clothing which was, unfortunately, from the Boy's, not the Men's, Department.

Now, sitting in homeroom, I looked at the boys milling around and felt pleased that I had exchanged my khakis and topsiders for jeans and sneakers. I was still the new kid, but at least I wasn't an obviously weird one. Maybe I could even fit in, if I found the right group. Which was definitely not the girls gathered near the teacher's desk. Not that I'd ever want to fit in with kids who gossiped and laughed so loudly. If they'd had a cauldron to stir, the girls would have been adding eye of newt and toe of frog.

All three were reasonably pretty and dressed fashionably in jeans and tight shirts. One of the girls--she wore her streaked blonde hair in a ponytail--dominated the conversation. Every time she whispered a comment to the others, they would explode in laughter. Soon, another girl entered the room, dressed similarly but, because of a slight plumpness, not to as great effect.

"Hi, Steph," the new entrant said to the ponytail girl.

I thought, 'Steph' as in Stephanie, as in Stephanie Stilton. Had to be, especially since homeroom assignments were done alphabetically, and I was an "R" and she was an "S."

"Hi, Brittany. Did you have a good summer?" asked Stephanie.

"Yeah, and you?"

"I can't complain. So, I take it you've given up cheerleading."

"What makes you say that?" asked Brittany.

"Well, try-outs are next week."

"I know. I've been working on my routines. I'll be ready."

Stephanie rolled her eyes at her two cohorts, "Well, somebody'd better lay off the Mrs. London brownies, big time."

The other two girls laughed. One of them held her hand out flat as if she were balancing something on it, "Oh, my darling brownie," she cooed, "I must bid you a fond farewell," and she kissed the air above her palm. The three girls laughed again. Brittany fled the room.

Another girl, this one with chin length hair, entered.

Stephanie said to her, "What did you do to your hair, Amanda?"

"Do you like it?" asked Amanda hopefully.

"Let's just say that it looks like your little brother cut it. Did he?"

Amanda sounded annoyed, "I'd like you to know that my mother took me all the way to Albany for this haircut. We didn't go to some dinky place in Saratoga."

"It may be hard to find an artist in Saratoga and hard to find a hack in Albany, but you and I have managed to do just that. I'd say your haircut will take about six months to grow out. Maybe you should consider home-schooling until then."

"The only reason I'd consider home-schooling is to get away from the likes of you," declared Amanda and, amidst gales of laughter, she moved to the back of the room to sit down.

A girl with black hair, big dark eyes, and light brown skin entered, wearing a shirt and pants emblazoned with "Abercrombie." I couldn't see what the objection would be here, but I felt certain Stephanie would find something.

"Hi, Radhika."

"Hi, Stephanie. Hi, Katie. Hi, Isabel." Isabel was the girl who had "kissed" the brownie, which meant that Katie was the other one.

Stephanie spoke, "New outfit?"

"Yeah. How could you tell?"

Stephanie turned to Katie and Isabel and said in a cloying voice, "Isn't that cute? Radhika still goes with her mommy to get a back-to-school outfit. My mommy used to get me a pretty new dress for the first day of school, and I'd wear a big bow in my hair. Radhika, you forgot to wear your big new bow."

Radhika laughed nervously along with the other three, although she didn't look very happy. Another girl walked in. This girl was really pretty, an all-American type with long blonde hair and blue eyes. She made the three witches look like Cinderella's stepsisters.

"Hi, Allison," said Stephanie.

Allison paused, as if considering whether to respond. Then she shrugged and said flatly, "Hi, Stephanie."

"I heard that you and Jared were an item this summer," said Stephanie.

"Emphasis on 'were,'" said Allison.

"I hear that's because, even on the hottest, steamiest nights, someone was frigid."

Allison's eyes narrowed. "Why don't you mind your own business?"

"It is my business when a friend of mine gets hurt. Why don't you enter a nunnery and leave the nice guys for the rest of us."

"You're welcome to all the guys like Jared any time," said Allison and, with a toss of her head, she turned and walked back to sit with Amanda.

The bell rang. It seemed more appropriate to mark the end of a boxing round than the beginning of homeroom. Our homeroom teacher, Mrs. Fitzgerald, entered, and everyone found a seat. Mrs. Fitzgerald was a pleasant-looking, middle aged woman with thick glasses that she continually had to push back into place. She started by taking attendance: she'd look at her list, call out the name, look up to put a face with the name while pushing up her glasses, smile at the new face, then look down to read the next name. Since everyone was new to the school, I thought I might escape the embarrassment of having my newness aired, but I was wrong.

When Mrs. Fitzgerald got to "Ross, Timothy" and I responded, "Here," she said, "I hope everyone will make an effort to say hello to our new student Timothy. Or do you prefer Tim?"

"Tim," I said, feeling my face redden.

She seemed oblivious to the distress she was causing me. "Well, welcome, Tim. We hope that you like Saratoga, in general, and the high school, in particular." Then, thank goodness, she moved on to "Russell, Allison."

During our homeroom period, which was extended for the first day, Mrs. Fitzgerald covered all sorts of basic rules and handed out class schedules. When she had finished covering the required material, she gave us five minutes "to chat quietly" among ourselves before we had to move to our shortened first classes. I figured I'd sit back and watch more of the Stephanie Stilton Show when I realized that she was

31

heading my way. I steeled myself for the onslaught. A public announcement that my clothes were new or that they were from the Gap or that I was too short to meet school safety standards or, worst of all, that my only pal in Saratoga was Caspar, the Friendly Ghost.

Instead, she came up to me and smiled. "Hi, I take it you're Timmy Ross."

"You take it right. I mean, yes I am."

"Timmy, if you're not doing anything Friday night, I'm having a few friends over to my house for a back-to-school party. We'd love you to join us."

Most of the kids in the room had stopped talking and were listening. I wasn't sure what to do. I didn't want to be associated with Stephanie, but I didn't want to immediately alienate a whole group in the high school. Some of her crowd might be nice, even if she wasn't. And it wasn't like I had any plans that night...or any other night.

"Sure, I'll come. Thanks," I said.

"Great. Nine o'clock at my house. You'll find the address in the phone book under *Doctor* Richard Stilton. Oh, and the party is by invitation only. No one will be admitted who hasn't been invited by me personally. So don't even think of bringing anyone else along."

Who would I bring? I didn't know anybody in Saratoga. Then I realized that the message wasn't for me, but for all the kids listening to our conversation. I wondered how many would be included and how many excluded. I had a feeling many more would be excluded because that was half the fun of having a party if you were Stephanie Stilton.

The bell rang, sounding the end of homeroom. Stephanie said, "Bye," and headed to the door. Mrs. Fitzgerald stopped Stephanie to thank her for being a model of kindness. Smiling sweetly, Stephanie said she was always happy to help a student in need.

I spent the rest of the school day in a daze, trying to find my way around the building. At least all the other ninth graders were in the same boat. When I got on the bus to go home, I expected a repeat solo journey and was shocked when Katie, the quiet one in Stephanie's cabal, plopped herself in the seat next to me. Herself and her huge backpack, which she put on the seat between us. I had one of those oversized backpacks at home, but I never used it. It was too cumbersome. I couldn't imagine what she had in that thing on the first day. I was crushed against the bus wall, but I wasn't complaining. It was too nice to have some company.

"Hi," she said, "I'm Katie Simon."

"I remember. From homeroom."

"And you're Timmy."

"Thanks for the reminder."

She looked at me funny, like she was trying to figure out if I was being serious or joking. She clearly couldn't decide, so chose to ignore the remark. "Are you excited about Stephanie's party? I can't wait. Her parties are always the best. Her mom buys all kinds of great things to eat, like chips and cheese puffs and pretzels. Oh, and M&Ms, plain and peanut. I'm not really allowed to eat any of it, because I have to watch my weight, but I like to smell it. Did you know that about seventy-five percent of taste comes from smell? That's why you can't taste things when you have a cold. Whenever I get a cold, I see it as an opportunity to fast. My mother's always like, 'You should *feed* a cold and starve a fever.' But I'm like, 'Who made that saying up? Some big, fat opera singer?' I mean, why take in calories when you can't enjoy the taste?"

I was starting to feel like I couldn't breathe, and not because of being squished by the big backpack. I had definitely misjudged this girl when I dubbed her "quiet." Maybe, because she was so talkative, she was forbidden to speak in Stephanie's presence and then, as soon as she was free, she had to make up for lost time. At least if I was going to have to listen to her, I could turn the subject to something of interest. "It was nice of Stephanie to invite me. To be honest, I was surprised."

"Oh, it's really an honor to be included in a Stilton party. Usually she's very choosy about the guest list, but in your case she was willing to make an exception. Her mom said that your father is actually interested in buying the horrible haunted house. He was so excited, he actually called her on Sunday to get more details. If he does buy it, Mrs. Stilton will make a lot of money. That house has been so impossible to sell that the owners are offering a special bonus on top of the commission. Mrs. Stilton said that, if Stephanie helps her out by being nice to you, she'll buy Stephanie an Audi convertible on her sixteenth birthday. I told Stephanie that her mother would probably do it anyway, but she said that it couldn't hurt to make her mother happy and to include you in one minor party at the beginning of the year. I mean, it's not like it's the Halloween party or the Thanksgiving party or the Christmas party. I especially love the Christmas party. Then Mrs. Stilton serves eggnog and sugar cookies and yule log. Eggnog is really good to sniff because it has a very distinctive smell. I think it's the cinnamon."

"You mean nutmeg," I said.

"Nutmeg?" she asked.

"People sprinkle eggnog with nutmeg, not cinnamon."

"Oh, I don't like nutmeg. I guess I'll have to stop sniffing eggnog. Anyway, the only thing I don't like about the Stilton parties is trying to figure out what to wear. Sometimes I think a casual skirt is the way to go, but then I feel more comfortable in dressy slacks. But if you wear slacks, you can't wear great shoes, although most of the time we end up taking off our shoes to dance, so what's the point in wearing great shoes? I'm always asking Stephanie what she's going to wear and she's like, 'This time, I'm definitely wearing a dress,' and then she goes and shows up in capris. It's really irritating. I swear she does it on purpose to make me wear a dress. Of course, one time she said she was wearing a dress

34

and I decided not to fall into her trap, so I wore a skort, and guess what? She actually wore a dress! It's like she's psychic, or something."

All of this talk about clothing was making me nervous. I didn't need to choose between a dress, a skirt, capris, or a skort--whatever that is--but I did need to find a suitable outfit. Now I had three good reasons not to go to the party. One, I didn't like the hostess. Two, the hostess didn't like me. And three, I had nothing to wear. Three strikes and you're out, right? I would call Stephanie on Friday afternoon with an excuse. If you clear your throat hard a few times, you get a pretty sore throat and don't have to lie. I wouldn't mention the party to my parents. I wasn't sure whether they'd push me to go, but I didn't want to take any chances.

Only it turned out that Mrs. Stilton had called my mom at work to "make sure Tommy would be at the party."

Really, she was calling to make sure that my parents, her potential customers, knew that the Stiltons were putting out the welcome mat. She also managed to mention that she had spoken to the sellers who were very eager to negotiate. For once, my mother had the presence of mind to ask a practical question: how would the boys be dressed at the party? The response: khakis, polo shirts and topsiders. I had a closet full of those. My fate was sealed.

Chapter Six

After the first two days of classes, at the teachers' insistence, the principal asked me to skip two grades in History and English and a grade in Spanish. I had already covered the material in middle school, and the teachers felt it was unfair to the other students, and themselves, that I knew all the answers. I stayed in ninth grade Math and Biology.

The hardest part of skipping grades was not the academic challenge--I was prepared for that--it was being two years younger than my classmates. Most of them were fully grown, making me seem painfully short and out of place. At least I didn't feel out of place all the time. After the first day, the adjoining seat on the bus ride to school was always filled by some boy or other. On the ride home, the seat was always filled by Katie. Within a few days of her company, I had learned more about dieting, make-up, cheerleading, and movie stars than I had in fourteen years. Not that I wanted to know about those subjects, but once Katie started talking, she didn't stop.

Each day, I was squished by Katie's overstuffed backpack which, I found out, was filled with clothes and shoes. It seems that, three years before, Katie and Radhika had worn the same outfit to school. Katie had sworn never to let it happen again and didn't mind the inconvenient backpack. I did. To reclaim adequate sitting space and my thoughts, I had to wait for Katie's stop. Then, in the last, quiet minutes of the ride, I would think of places where the attic key might be hidden because, as soon as I walked into the empty house, I was free to explore.

On the first day of searching, I checked the attic door area, but when I came up empty, I tried to think historically. A big, old house would have had more than front and back door keys. It would have had keys to all the rooms containing valuables, and those keys would have been held together on a ring, kept by the mistress. The ring of keys would have been stored near the centers of activity, either in the basement or in the kitchen. I would start in the basement and work my way up. On the second day, I propped open the basement door with a phone book--I had read too many books where a door slams shut--then carefully climbed down the steep, narrow stairs.

At the bottom, I found a small room which passed through to several others, all of them grimy and neglected. An uncovered light bulb hung down in the center of each room, leaving the corners dark. Using my flashlight, I saw, in the last room, something glimmer. I hurried over and discovered, hanging on a hook, a large metal ring holding two old-fashioned skeleton keys. I couldn't believe my luck! I grabbed them, wiping off the cobwebs on my pants, then as fast as I could, I ran through the basement, up the basement stairs, up the first floor stairs, up the second floor stairs, to the attic door.

I was breathing hard and my heart was pounding as I tried the first key. It didn't fit, but maybe that was because my hand was so unsteady. I tried again. Nothing. I tried the second key. It fit into the lock. I thought I would burst. Then I turned the key. Nothing. Maybe the lock was jammed or the key was bent. I pulled the key out and checked it in the dim light. It looked fine, straight and clean. I rubbed it on my pants, just to be sure. I tried the lock again, but the key wouldn't turn. I took the key out and turned the flashlight on it.

Onto the long tubular barrel, the word "Wine" was scratched, presumably indicating that the key opened the wine cellar. I checked the other key. That one had the word "Still" scratched on it. What the heck did that mean? Then it came to me: "still" was short for "stillroom" where tonics and perfumes were distilled in old houses. I knew this because one of the many Victorian homes I had been dragged to in London was Charles Dickens'. That home had a stillroom located in the basement near the wine cellar and the wash room. The tour guide had said that, by Dickens' time in the mid-1800s, the stillroom had been converted to serve as storage space. Stillrooms had gone out of fashion, but Chatsworth Mansion had been built with one.

I indulged myself in a groan of disappointment. I had found these keys in the basement because they went to rooms in the basement.

"Great thinking, Tim," I said aloud, my voice heavy with sarcasm and frustration, "You're a regular genius." I banged on the door a few times, working myself up. "Where the hell is the key?" I shouted, but, of course, nobody answered.

I forced myself to calm down and, since I was all the way upstairs, I checked around once more for the key. I shone my flashlight around the attic door and inside the nearest closets. Nothing. Slowly, I went down the three flights of stairs to put the key ring back on the hook.

* * *

I have to admit, I was feeling pretty discouraged and I might have given up, but that night I had a dream that got me back on track. Here's how my dream went: I heard a voice calling my name while I was asleep in my bed. The "Tim, Tim" was barely audible, so I got up and followed the sound. It grew louder and louder as I headed up the stairs to the attic door. When I reached the door, the calling stopped, and the door opened automatically, as if someone on the other side had been waiting for me. I should have been afraid, but I felt safe and welcomed. The staircase was well lit, and I eagerly climbed up. At the top, the light was dim, but my eyes adjusted, and I saw that the attic was large and filled with big, old trunks. I didn't know which one to open first, and then I realized it didn't matter because they were all mine. I made myself walk through the maze of trunks to the farthest one in the back and slowly raised its lid. I had barely caught a glimpse, when I let the lid bang shut. The gleam of the jewels inside had hurt my eyes. I reopened the trunk, being careful to avert my gaze. Then I moved to the next trunk and opened it cautiously. It was packed with glittering gold doubloons. I left its lid open. I made my way around the room, opening the lids of every trunk to reveal the breath-taking treasures inside. When I had finished, the room was no longer dark, but brilliantly lit from the exposed, glowing treasures. I must be the richest person on the planet, I thought. And then I started to laugh, harder and harder, and I must have really been laughing, because I woke myself up with the noise.

The weirdest thing was, long after the sound of laughter left my head, I could hear the faintest whisper of someone calling my name. It was as though that part of the dream had been real. But I knew nothing in the dream could be real. Mr. Henry had said that, over the years, people had been up to the attic. Big trunks full of treasure would not have been missed. Still, I couldn't shake the feeling that I was supposed to go up to the attic, that someone was waiting up there to give me something valuable.

* * *

I returned to investigating with renewed vigor. Unfortunately, searches of the dining room, the living room, the kitchen, and the library were all unsuccessful. It made me wish I were back living in the tiny Scarsdale apartment where finding a lost object would take an hour, tops. But, of course, if I lived in Scarsdale, I wouldn't need to find the key. My muddled thinking was a clear indication that I was spending too much time with Katie.

* * *

Before I knew it, Friday night had arrived. When, as instructed, I looked up *Doctor* Richard Stilton's address, I discovered that Stephanie lived in a new development down by Saratoga Lake. It was a few miles away, which meant biking wasn't an option. I suggested to my parents that I not attend.

"What?" said my dad, "And deprive all the fairest maidens in the land of a chance to dance with the handsome prince? I think not."

"What your father's trying to say is that you should go. We'll drive you there and pick you up," said my mom.

"But why should I go? We all agree that Ellen Stilton is evil incarnate. And, I'm telling you, her daughter is irrefutable evidence that human cloning has been achieved by mad scientists in secret laboratories."

"That may well be," said my dad, "But you need to get out more. Meet people. Talk. Dance. Laugh."

"There won't be anyone at this party who I can talk, dance, or laugh with. I've seen enough of the crowd to know that I'll be wasting my time," I argued.

"If you're right, you'll go this one time, and never again," said my mom.

"That's already guaranteed," I said. "Stephanie only invited me this once to butter you and Dad up for her mother. Mrs. Stilton thinks that you're seriously interested in buying this place, and she's drooling over the commission already."

"Well, even if their motives are impure, the outcome could be good. Maybe Cinderella will attend and meet her handsome prince," said my mom. "You can't miss important opportunities. You've got to get out there and beat the bushes."

"Just because you and Dad have been together since junior high, doesn't mean that I'm over-the-hill at the age of fourteen."

40

My parents were unusually eager for me to be paired off because they had been the proverbial boy-and-girl next door. My Ross grandparents had moved into their house in the spring of 1960 and two weeks later my Cohen grandparents moved in next door. Both couples had two year olds, and neither couple ever had another child. The two couples became best friends and their children were constant companions. By the time my mom and dad were thirteen, it was clear that they would never part. The only problem with having parents who grow up together is that, in some ways, they never grow up. Experts call such cases "arrested development," which always makes me think of a policeman snapping psychological handcuffs on the thirteen-year-old versions of my mom and dad, as he says, "You have the right to remain immature. Any responsibility you accept can and will be held against you."

My father said, "Seriously, Tiny Tim, we know you're nervous. You have every reason to be nervous. It's tough to walk in on a group where everyone knows and likes each other and you're the outsider. My advice is for you to go to that party and be yourself. Make sure that everybody notices you. The other kids may not understand you, they may not like you, they may even despise you, but you'll walk out of that room with your soul intact and your head held high."

This speech was supposed to make me feel better about going to the party, but it was having the opposite effect.

Then my dad added, as if a light bulb had gone on over his head, "I've got a great idea! To break the ice, why don't you dig out the old cowboy hat and wear it? Then you can tell everybody about the good ole days in Montana."

Thanks, dad, I thought, why don't I just wear the cowboy hat and a skort. That ought to break the ice. Or better yet, I could wear the cowboy hat and nothing else.

Before my dad got any more "great ideas," I ran upstairs to get changed. I could have put up more of a battle, but this party meant a lot to my parents. They felt guilty about up-

41

rooting me every couple of years and wanted me to make friends. I couldn't disappoint them, so I resigned myself to spending two hours eating...what had Katie said?...pretzels, cheese puffs, chips and M&Ms while watching the scene. It didn't exactly sound like torture. But one thing was certain, I was not going to call attention to myself.

* * *

As I got out of the car at the Stiltons, I said, "Remember, deadline at twenty-three hundred, same location." That limited my captivity to exactly an hour and a half. Given their obsession with punctuality, my parents would be there.

"Roger that, son," said dad, and he gave me a thumbs up.

Walking up the path, I got a good look at the Stilton house. It was big and it was ugly. Newly constructed, it had styles of architecture from different eras thrown together. As if the jumble weren't bad enough, the house dwarfed its plot of land. There was barely any space between the huge house and its neighbors, which were also designed from an architectural smorgasbord.

After passing through twin sets of thick, round columns, I reached the front door, a dark wood eyesore with etched glass panels on either side. In comparison, Chatsworth Mansion with its Victorian integrity seemed surprisingly appealing.

Chapter Seven

At least you could say this about the Stiltons: they were consistent. The inside of the house was as ugly as the outside. The walls of the large entryway were painted pink to match the pink marble floor. I had no idea where to go in the Land-of-Cotton-Candy, but the kid ahead of me moved with purpose, so I followed. As we headed to the back of the house, I got a peek at the dining room which was all floral, the living room which was all white, and the library which was all plaid. My point man disappeared through a doorway. When I got there, I discovered a carpeted staircase that led down to the dark, noisy basement.

The basement was a large, finished space, sparsely furnished with what had to be rejects from the upstairs rooms: two white chairs, a plaid loveseat, and a round table covered with a floral tablecloth. Better to be a reject in the basement than the attic, I thought. And, once again, as they so often did, my thoughts turned to the Chatsworth attic. Where was that damned key? I had looked in every logical place in the house. Maybe I needed to look outside. I wished I could start looking now, but I couldn't, so I tried to focus on the scene at hand.

Kids, some of whom I recognized from school, were standing in groups or sitting on the furniture. Radhika stood with two other girls in a corner. I was surprised that she had made the cut. It was clear that Stephanie didn't like her and only kept her around to torment her. I guess that Radhika's willingness to be a punching bag kept those party invitations flowing.

I felt awkward standing alone, but I didn't see a place to sit down. Maybe I should have come earlier to snag an upholstered piece. My late arrival, however, had been purposeful; I had dragged my heels to avoid being the first through the door, which my dad would have happily arranged.

I was trying to decide on my next move when Stephanie came over. Thanks to Katie's influence, I noted that she was wearing a white mini-skirt and a black halter top.

"Hi, Timmy, I see that you made it."

"Yup, wild horses couldn't keep me away," I said. Which was oddly true, since I had come by car and not by horse.

She said, "I'm surprised that you ever want to go out. I mean, if I lived in a house as great as yours, I don't think I'd ever leave. It was so smart of your parents to buy the mansion."

I played dumb. "Oh, my parents haven't bought the mansion. They're just renting it."

"Really? Well, you should tell them to buy it immediately. I hear from my mother that there's lots of interest from other buyers, and the price is sure to go up by the spring."

"Thanks for letting us know. That's awfully thoughtful. I'll be sure to tell my parents...as soon as they get out of the penitentiary."

She didn't acknowledge my last comment. It wasn't part of the script in her head. "Great. Well, I'd better go mingle." She walked away without waiting for a response.

I said to her back, my words lost in the loud music, "Have fun mingling. I'm sure you're a first-class mingler. I would mangle a mingle."

I realized I'd better stop in case anyone was watching. They'd think I was talking to myself which, technically, I was. Out of the corner of my eye, I spotted buried treasure: an empty plaid bench in a dark, quiet corner. I skillfully maneuvered my way around the various groups of minglers and sat down. Reaching over to a nearby table laden with snacks, I grabbed a bowl of cheese puffs and set to work. After a few minutes of crunching, I noticed Katie headed my way. I prayed that she wouldn't see me. Luckily, her radar was locked onto something, blocking out everything else. Arriving at the snack table, she looked around to see if anybody was looking. Satisfied that she was alone and unobserved, she stuck her nose in the bowl of peanut M&Ms. I made a mental note not to eat any peanut M&Ms at the Stiltons', although I'm quite partial to them.

When Katie came up for air, I considered calling to her, but I concluded I wasn't that desperate. At least not yet. I still had plenty of cheese puffs to keep me company. By the way, Katie was wearing black slacks. All the other girls were wearing some form of skirts or dresses. No wonder Katie had sought comfort in the smell of chocolate and peanuts.

Stephanie had bossed her guests away from the center of the room to its edges and then had insisted that they return to the center to dance. A few half-hearted couples obliged. This improved the quality of my surveillance. I couldn't overhear any conversations, but I could watch the dance floor. Most of the dancers, especially the boys, were awful, but amusing. Then I noticed this one girl, wearing a pale green dress with a full skirt. She was an amazing dancer. Once you started looking at her, you couldn't take your eyes off of her. I don't know much about dancing, but every movement looked graceful and she had a lot of variety, unlike most of the kids who had just one or two moves.

If I'm totally honest, part of the girl's allure had nothing to do with her dancing. She was great looking. Not in the way Allison Russell, the all-American blonde from homeroom, was great looking because she fit the standard; this girl was great looking because she didn't fit the standard. I'm sure a lot of kids wouldn't see it, but the more I looked, the more beautiful she seemed. In the dim light, this girl's pale skin seemed to glow. Her small, red mouth was smiling with the pleasure of dancing. Her eyes were smiling, too. Her nose, which had a small bump near the top, was thin and distinguished. But the most incredible thing about this girl was her hair. She had tons of it, light brown and wavy, the top layer of which she had pulled back into a barrette, so it was off her face, but still hung down past her shoulders. She looked like a girl in one of my mother's posters by the Victorian painter Dante Gabriel Rossetti.

The song ended and some boys in the far corner were screaming and carrying on. I looked over to see what all the ruckus was about. It was an intense arm-wrestling match, with supporters for both sides chanting encouragement. When another song came on, I looked back at the dance floor and was crushed to find my Pre-Raphaelite maiden gone.

"Hi." The voice startled me. I looked to my left where the sound came from. Standing next to the bench was the girl. I was totally dumbfounded. She waited patiently through the awkward pause, then said, "You're awfully quiet, aren't you?"

Since I didn't want her to leave, I forced myself to speak. "I'm trying to retain my air of mystery."

She smiled. "You could do that better wearing a trench coat and fedora."

I smiled, too. "I was thinking more along the lines of a checked cape, a deerstalker, and a calabash pipe."

"Well, Sherlock Holmes, have you figured out who I am?" she asked.

"You're the fairy princess who's come to save me from the depths of hell."

"Close, but we fairy princesses aren't allowed to save anyone. Too much heavy lifting, and we're unionized. Still, we are allowed to show people how to save themselves."

"I eagerly await your instructions."

"You start by saying your name, then you put out your hand to shake."

"I'm Tim Ross." I put out my hand. "But I must warn you: you shake this hand at your peril. I've been eating cheese puffs for the last fifteen minutes with no napkin."

She reached into the bowl, took a cheese puff, rolled it around in her fingers, and ate it. "Now we're evenly matched." She stuck out her hand and shook mine. "Emma Green, at your service." She gestured to the empty space on the bench. "Mind if I sit?"

I don't mind, I thought. And by "don't mind" I meant there wasn't anything I wanted more in the world. By way of response, I moved as far as I could, opening up more space. I was hanging off the edge, but it seemed to be my lot in life to be scrunched. She sat down.

"What brings you to these parts?" she asked.

"I came to Saratoga for the waters," I was actually making a reference to the movie *Casablanca*, knowing that I was just amusing myself. Except I wasn't.

She laughed and delivered the famous next line, "The waters? What waters? We're in the desert."

I finished the exchange, "I was misinformed."

We both laughed.

She asked, "But, really, you're new here, aren't you?"

"I'm afraid so. Is that an asset or a liability?"

"Definitely an asset. I'm tired of all the same old faces. I've known most of these kids since kindergarten."

"That's funny, because I'm tired of unfamiliar faces. I wish I could hang out with kids who I'd known for years."

"Moved a lot, huh?"

"Let no grass grow beneath the Ross feet," I said.

"Tell me where you've lived and what it was like."

"Believe me, you don't want to hear that long story."

"And why not? I've got an elegant resting place, plenty of sustenance...." She took another cheese puff from the bowl. "...And a desire to avoid the dance floor where my feet were getting crushed. If you've got the story, I've got the ears."

"Well, don't blame me if you get bored. You've been duly warned," I said. Then I plunged into the tale of my wandering life. Once I started, I couldn't stop. I was afraid that my monologue was on par with Katie's blabbing: fascinating to the speaker and irksome to the listener. But Emma gave no such indication; she kept nodding and asking questions and reacting appropriately with smiles and frowns and laughter and sighs.

When I had relayed the outline of my fourteen years, I begged her for her life story. She protested that her story was painfully boring compared to mine, but I insisted. And, of course, she was wrong. Both her parents were lawyers. Her father worked in Albany, her mother in Saratoga. She had two younger siblings, a chess fanatic brother and a tennis fanatic sister. She loved school, particularly reading and writing, and was an excellent student. Now, here's the interesting part: she was a ballet dancer. Not one of those I-take-class-once-a-week-to-stay-in-shape girls, but a passionate dancer who only took Sundays off. It turns out that Saratoga isn't only known for its waters and its horse racing, it is also known for world-class ballet. Every summer since the 1960's, The New York City Ballet has spent a few weeks dancing at the performing arts center. For the past four years, Emma had danced kids' parts with the company. No wonder she was so impressive on the Stilton dance floor.

"And the best part of ballet is," she said, "I have a life separate from all of this." She gestured at the crowd.

"Aren't these your friends?" I asked, hoping that the answer would be no.

"I've never been invited to a Stilton party before in my life. I almost didn't come...I didn't think there'd be anyone here like you."

"That's funny because my parents had to drag me here. I didn't want to go to a party where I wasn't wanted."

"Wait. Why were you invited if you weren't wanted?"

"Stephanie Stilton only invited me because she thinks that

my parents will buy a house from her mother. Although Stephanie knows me from homeroom, she's remained oblivious to my captivating charm, my rapier wit, and my dashing good looks."

"Stephanie Stilton will never really see you. She doesn't see anybody. Maybe it's from spending so much time gazing in the mirror. Anyway, I'm glad to hear that you're not aching to be part of this group. I'm not sure how many of these parties I could take, even with the excellent provisions." She ate another cheese puff.

A shadow fell across our faces. We looked up to see, standing over us, a muscular, handsome guy.

"Let's dance," he said to Emma.

"Um, ok, in a minute," she said, flustered. "I just want to finish my conversation with Tim."

"But I want to dance now," he said firmly.

"Then why don't you ask somebody else and when you're done, I'll be ready. Look, there's Katie." She pointed. "Nobody's dancing with her."

"But I don't want to dance with Katie. I want to dance with you. I know you must be pissed off that I'm so late, but don't ruin the rest of the evening. Now, are you coming or not?"

"Not. I'm finishing my very enjoyable conversation with Tim."

At first the guy looked astonished; then he looked angry. He stormed across the floor, stopping to whisper something to Stephanie who stood by the stairs. Although he stomped up the stairs, their thick carpeting undermined the intended dramatic effect. After Stephanie watched him ascend, she turned her gaze on us and headed our way.

"Uh oh, I think we are in trouble," whispered Emma to me. Only it wasn't "we" in trouble, just me in trouble.

The room had suddenly gotten very quiet; a song had ended, but no one put another one on, and now all eyes were fixed on our corner. When Stephanie arrived, she said quietly to Emma, "Jared is waiting for you in the kitchen. As you can tell, he's very upset. As your hostess, I'm asking you to go to him."

"Sure," said Emma, standing up. She took another cheese puff, quickly rubbed it in her hand, popped it in her mouth, and held out her hand to shake mine. "Thanks, Tim, for a lovely evening. We'll have to do it again sometime soon."

While we were shaking hands, I thought she might have squeezed mine, but I couldn't be sure. Then she moved across the floor and up the stairs.

Once Emma was gone, Stephanie turned on me, full blast. "How dare you try to ruin my party?! Who are you?! You're a nobody. Oh wait, you're only half a nobody. You're a freak, living in a freak house. What made me think that you could mingle with normal people? I knew deep-down that it was a mistake to invite you, but I'm way too nice. Well, I'm through with being Mrs. Nice. Let's see how you like Mrs. Mean."

I had a strong urge to laugh, but I was pretty sure it would just fan the flames of Stephanie's fury. Humor didn't seem the way to go; I went with quiet dignity and said, "I can tell when I'm not wanted. I'll be leaving now."

This pronouncement, while appropriately dramatic, was no big sacrifice. I had recently checked my watch, and it was close to eleven. My parents would be arriving any minute, might even have arrived given their tendency to be hyper-punctual, so I could make a grand exit without being inconvenienced.

"Good riddance," said Stephanie, and she ran across the floor and up the stairs, presumably to mediate the melo-drama in the kitchen.

I waited until she was gone to head out. At the stairs, there was a bit of a bottleneck, and I had to look a guy named Gary, from my math class, right in the eye.

Gary shook his head and said, "Gosh, Tim, you shouldn't have done that."

50

"Done what?" I wasn't being sarcastic. I had no idea what I'd done. I hadn't even said a single word to Jared. Emma had done all the talking.

"Tried to steal Jared's girl," he said.

"Jared's girl? She's not Jared's girl," I protested.

"Who told you that?" he asked.

"Nobody," I answered. Well, technically she did...by her behavior, but it didn't seem gentlemanly to say so.

"But everybody knows she's Jared's girl," he asserted.

I replied, "I was misinformed."

Chapter Eight

Although I had soundly rejected my dad's advice to call attention to myself at the party, I had inadvertently followed it exactly, even down to walking out despised by everyone. Everyone, that is, except the one person I cared about. I was pretty sure that Emma liked me, and I was hoping that her defiance at the party would be the breaking point of her relationship, if there was one, with Jared.

I had to focus on warm, happy thoughts because, once I got outside, I was freezing. The temperature had dropped precipitously while I was inside, and my parents were nowhere in sight. I checked my watch by the street light and discovered I was ten minutes early. My parents would pull up any minute, and I certainly wasn't going back inside. I walked briskly up and down the sidewalk with my arms wrapped around my body.

My parents finally arrived ten minutes after their deadline, twenty minutes after I had become Nanook of the North. I climbed in and made them crank up the heat. Both mom and dad apologized for their tardiness. They had come to the development early, but had taken a wrong turn and gotten lost in the maze of streets. It wasn't until my mother had spotted me on the sidewalk that their search had ended.

As soon as they established that I was fine, they asked if I had enjoyed myself. I had to think for a minute before I responded, weighing the pleasure of meeting Emma against the misery of being humiliated, and I decided that I was glad I went and told my parents so. They grinned at each other across the front seat as if to say, "We should never have worried about our little man. He may be shy, but everyone who knows him, loves him." I hastily declared, though, that I didn't want to go to any more Stilton parties. I didn't bother to mention that, even if I had wanted to, I wouldn't be invited.

The next morning, I awoke with a rotten cold, but it didn't really matter since I had no weekend plans. At least the cold was a good excuse to stay in bed and sleep. Whenever I was awake, I was jumping out of my skin, wondering what had happened between Emma and Jared. At one point, I looked up "Green" in the phonebook. There were about twelve numbers. Since I didn't know her street or her father's name, I had to be patient.

There was another reason I didn't hotly pursue the trail: maybe Emma really was Jared's girl and was just being nice at the party because she felt sorry for me. You could tell that Emma was a warm person; maybe I had misread her general warmth for particular warmth. And if she was going out with Jared, I definitely wasn't her type. He was tall; I was small. He was brawny; I was scrawny. He was the strong, silent type; I was the cut-up, loquacious type. At least, with Emma I had been. I tried to think about something else, but even the attic key failed to distract me.

Luckily, a distraction presented itself on Sunday morning in the form of Mr. Henry who showed up bearing a couple of big boxes from Mrs. London's Bakery. He had brought us an assortment of scones, croissants and brownies as a house-warming gift. I made the necessary introductions, and my mom went to make some tea while the rest of us sat down in the living room. I tried a bit of scone but, not being able to taste it, decided to save the treats for when I recovered. Katie was nuts, but she was right that you shouldn't waste delicious food on a cold.

Although Mr. Henry hadn't known I was sick, he had, fortunately, brought along a non-edible offering. He took a book out of a plastic bag, saying, "This is an oldie, but goodie. I knew I had it, but I couldn't remember where I had put it. If my wife were still alive, she would have found it immediately. But I shouldn't complain too much. Burrowing for this drifter caused me to find a bunch of other missing things, like my sunglasses and my stamp collection."

He passed me the book. The cover read *Saratoga Revealed*. He continued, "Although this book is long out of print, I think you'll find the photo on page 29 relevant."

He had marked the page with a slip of paper, and I turned to it. There was a photo of Chatsworth Mansion, sitting on the hill, the trees not quite as tall and full as I knew them. While I recognized the structure of the house, its overall appearance was very different.

"This is incredible. The house looks so much better." I said, passing the book to my parents.

"I agree," said Mr. Henry. "Until pretty recently, it was always painted a lovely light brown with white trim. Of course, you can't fully appreciate the color in the black and white photo, but you can see that the house wasn't a monstrosity."

"But why would anyone paint it dark gray?" asked my father.

I spoke up, "Mr. Henry told me that the house was used as a bed and breakfast for fans of haunted houses. The dark gray made the house creepier."

"Well I think the house deserves to be restored to its original glory," declared my mother.

Mr. Henry said, "It would be wonderful, wouldn't it, but difficult. First, you would have to get permission from the National Registry. And second, you'd have to spend a pretty penny on painting a house this size. If you were the owners, I would urge the project, but it's not for renters. Unfortunately, the current owners won't do anything; they have too much money tied up in the place already."

"Even if we can't do much, we appreciate your calling the matter to our attention," said my dad, offering the book back to Mr. Henry.

He refused to take it. "The book is yours to keep. It may come in handy someday."

After Mr. Henry left, I crawled back into bed and frittered away the rest of the day by shooting foam-ball baskets, reading books, and day-dreaming about outings I would take with Emma.

* * *

On Monday morning, I awoke feeling improved, but not fully recovered. My mother offered to let me stay home for the day but, while I normally would have jumped at such an opportunity, I refused. I couldn't wait to find out what had happened at the Stiltons.

From the bus ride, I got the feeling that I should have stayed home. No one sat next to me. I tried to brush it off as no one wanting to sit next to a kid with a runny, red nose. Walking through the hallway wasn't great either. A football player knocked into me and said, looking over my head, "Sorry, Bite Size, I didn't see you." Then he and his buddy laughed. Another big guy wasn't as affable. He plowed into me, then yelled at me, "for getting underfoot."

In homeroom, everyone pretended I didn't exist. I felt like a ghost walking among the living. I guess that some kids were mad at me for ruining the Stilton party, some were mad at me for going at all, and everybody was intimidated by Stephanie.

Before the teacher arrived, Stephanie made a point of loudly telling Katie and Isabel, "I feel so relieved that everything worked out Friday night. I mean, if my party had caused Jared and Emma to break up, I would never have forgiven myself. Although, obviously, the person who really shouldn't be forgiven shall remain nameless." She nodded her head in my direction.

This was clearly a staged performance for the benefit of the homeroom crowd and me. Katie and Isabel had slept over Stephanie's house on Friday night--on Thursday's bus ride Katie had debated whether to pack a nightgown, a nightshirt, or pajamas--so I was sure Stephanie had already shared the information with the cabal.

Stephanie continued, "I still can't believe that, after I put myself out to do something nice for someone, he would try to steal my best friend's girl. As if anyone could compete with Jared, who's the starting quarterback even though he's only a sophomore. Not to mention that he's tall and movie-star-handsome. If anyone has reason to feel secure about himself, it's Jared. It's just that no one wants to have things going on behind their back."

For once, Katie spoke up. "That is so true. Remember the time Robert came over to our table in the cafeteria and asked me out and I said "yes" and then, like two hours later, he came over to me in math class and said he had just been kidding and that he didn't want to take me out. When I bugged him about why he changed his mind, he admitted that someone had told him that I was crazy and would stalk him if he ever tried to break up with me. I never could get him to tell me who said that, but I sure wish I knew."

Stephanie turned red; she had guilt written all over her. Out of pure malice, she must have scared off Katie's suitor. Stephanie hissed, "Be quiet, Katie. We're talking about Jared and Emma, not about you. And I'm happy to say that, thanks to my speedy intervention, everything is fine. Jared couldn't stop thanking me yesterday for making everything right, and now he and Emma are happier and more in love than ever before." She actually heaved a contented sigh. She was really selling it.

I hoped that her information was as false as her delivery, but I had no way of knowing. I had no classes with Emma, and the school was big. Plus, Emma never hung around after school. She had told me that everyday she rushed from

56

school to the ballet studio. Still, even though it was futile, I looked for Emma all day and found myself really bumping into people and, deservedly, getting yelled at. By three o'clock, I couldn't wait to get out.

On the bus ride home, no one sat with me. At least Katie wasn't filling my ear with chatter, and I was able to overhear a few conversations about Jared and Emma. There seemed to be a consensus that they were still an item. My heart sank. I could take being abused by Stephanie, but being rejected by Emma really hurt. An hour's conversation didn't entitle me to her never-ending devotion, but I had hoped that it would earn me another opportunity to talk.

When I got home, I was sorely tempted to escape back into my bed. But it was a sunny, warm afternoon, and Friday night's chill was a vivid reminder that winter comes early and stays late in Saratoga. I willed myself to stop moping over Emma--I couldn't let one hour of my life ruin every other hour--and went outside to search for the key.

I started with the tree trunks near the house. In some big knots, I found quite a few acorns stored by squirrels, but no key. Then I moved to the overgrown garden on the house's right hand side. I had come armed and ready to dig...with a large metal spoon from the kitchen.

I cut into the dirt carefully, making furrows around the plants which must have reseeded themselves year after year. I hadn't done any digging for ages--not since my California days--and I was enjoying it. The sun warmed my back, and my nose cleared enough that I could smell the dirt's earthy scent. I had almost forgotten that I was on a mission when my spoon hit something metallic.

I forced myself to keep calm and to dig a little faster. When I extracted the metal object, with dirt still clinging to it, I saw that it wasn't the right shape for a key. It was a flat rectangle, about three inches long, an inch wide and a quarter of an inch thick. I rubbed off the dirt and read, engraved on one side, the word "basil." Whoever took care of the garden had used tags to mark the plants' placement each year. Sure enough, as I widened my dig, I found many more markers, including ones for sage, thyme, parsley, mint, lemon balm, chamomile, echinacea, chive, wormwood, and lavender. This must have been the herb garden for use in the kitchen and stillroom.

As cool as the markers were, they weren't the key, and I was about to give up when my spoon hit another, larger object. Once again, I picked up the pace. Only this time, instead of being too small, the object was too big. It was a pair of antique thin-wire spectacles. I cleaned off one arm and held it up in the sunlight. Just as I had suspected, it was marked 14k, meaning 14 carat gold, which made the glasses pretty valuable. They weren't in good condition, though. One round frame had no glass in it and the other frame's glass was broken in two. It was unlikely that the owner, possibly Chatsworth himself, had tossed away such a necessary item, but it could have fallen out of his pocket during a stroll.

Maybe the spectacles were Chatsworth's way of communicating with me. Maybe he was telling me to start seeing more clearly.

Chapter Nine

On Monday, school had been pretty terrible, but it was just a preview of many more terrible days. At least on Monday, I had harbored hope for the future. As the days passed and I had no word from Emma, I grew more depressed. I desperately wanted to talk to her, but I also desperately wanted to avoid being in a Jared-inflicted body cast.

Finally, a few weeks later, I ran into Emma on my way to the cafeteria. As I turned the corner of the hallway, I knocked into someone, sending a notebook skittering across the floor. Before registering whom my victim was, I went to retrieve the notebook and began apologizing.

I heard Emma laugh and say, "Tim, I've been hoping to bump into you, but not literally."

I stood up to hand back the notebook and, when I looked in her eyes, my stomach flip-flopped. She was waiting. I had to speak.

I said, "It's really nice to see you. How have you been?"

"Busy. Lots of ballet and schoolwork and...you know."

I did know. Jared. She continued, "And you? How's Saratoga treating you?"

What was I supposed to say? That I had made no friends? That I was as welcome as rabies?

I said, "Hmm, you always ask for the long stories. If you have the time, I'd love to tell you. I'm heading to the cafeteria. We could go grab something to eat...and by 'something to eat' I mean a barely palatable substance containing lots of calories."

"Oh, Tim, I wish I could, but...um..." She didn't have to finish her sentence. Coming down the other end of the hallway was Jared and two of his raucous football friends. I fled. I didn't want to get beaten up, and even if Jared didn't resort to violence, I didn't want to see him give Emma the inevitable kiss hello. But I didn't flee to the cafeteria. My appetite was gone.

* * *

Some of my schoolmates, especially Jared's football teammates, continued to give me a hard time. The nicknames "Bite Size" and "Short Stuff" had caught on, and many kids seemed to have forgotten my real name. Nobody cared about the party mess anymore; they had just gotten into the habit of harassing me and didn't bother to break it. Back in Scarsdale where I was ignored, I had wondered whether it would be preferable to be disliked, just to get some attention. Now I knew the answer: it was much better to be ignored.

* * *

During the next couple of months, I focused on getting through the days. I still looked for the attic key, but with less enthusiasm. It had probably been lost long ago, and I would have to content myself with living in the house without getting to the top floor. My free time was spent doing homework, reading mysteries, playing indoor basketball, riding my bike, visiting Mr. Henry, playing computer games, and wishing for something special to happen so I wouldn't have to engage in all the preceding activities.

The days were getting shorter, the weather cooler, the leaves turned color and then fell to the ground. My mom bought two big pumpkins from the Saturday Farmer's Market and carved scary faces in them. Exactly a week later, it was Halloween. Mr. Henry counseled my parents not to buy candy for trick-or-treaters. Because the houses on our street were set far apart, almost no costumed kiddies ever came. And the few who did come to our neighborhood never rang the bell at Chatsworth Mansion. Between the treacherous driveway and the ghostly reputation, everyone avoided the mansion on Halloween.

For the entire week before Halloween, the kids at school had been buzzing about parties, costumes, and planned pranks. Halloween seemed to be an equal opportunity holiday: anyone with a sheet and a dream could participate. I kept hanging on the fringes of conversations, hoping someone would invite me to a party. I even dug out my old cowboy hat, some worn jeans, a long-sleeved checked shirt, and a bandana, just in case. I shouldn't have bothered, though. Saturday afternoon arrived, and there was no eleventh hour reprieve.

To add insult to injury, my parents had been invited to a "come as your favorite writer" party by one of my mom's Skidmore colleagues. My mom was so excited that she drove to Albany to rent Victorian garb for herself and my dad, or I should say, for Charlotte Bronte and Charles Dickens.

Late Saturday afternoon, as she was getting decked out in her pantaloons and hoop skirt, my mom couldn't contain her joy. With her door open, she sang at the top of her lungs, "The Sun, The Moon and I" from Gilbert and Sullivan's *Mikado* in which the heroine boasts that her natural beauty is as fine as the sun and moon's. Of course, my mother reveled in the Victorian words and music.

> The sun, whose rays
> Are all ablaze
> With ever-living glory,
> Does not deny
> His majesty--
> He scorns to tell a story!
> He don't exclaim,
> "I blush for shame,
> So kindly be indulgent."
> But, fierce and bold,

61

In fiery gold,
He glories all effulgent!

She stopped for breath, and I called out from my room where I was lying on my bed, trying to read, "Mom, all the windows are shattering. Replacement costs will be staggering. If you want to send me to college, you'd better stop!" She ignored me and pressed on.

I mean to rule the earth,
As he the sky--
We really know our worth,
The sun and I!
I mean to rule the earth,
As he the sky--
We really know our worth,
The sun and I!

Another break and I called, "Mom, dogs are howling and are threatening to commit hari kari."

This time, thank goodness, she stopped, but only because she had finished dressing and had come to my door to show off her hoop skirt by twirling around to make it flare out.

She said, "Timmy, I'm really sorry that you can't come with us tonight."

"That's ok, Mom, you go and have a good time."

"Is there anything I can get you? Something to eat? Something to drink? Another rousing chorus of Gilbert and Sullivan?"

"Please just go and put me out of my misery."

"Well, if there's candy at the party, we'll be sure to bring some home. Don't forget, we expect to be out late tonight, so don't wait up." She walked over to my bed and gave me a kiss on the top of my head. Then she and my dad left for an evening of cocktails, dinner, and literary charades.

I must have dozed off, because I was asleep when I heard the phone ringing. It was still pretty early, but had already gotten dark, and I stumbled through the hall to my parents' room to pick up.

"Hello," I said.

"Hello. May I please speak to Timmy?" I recognized the voice at once; it was Katie.

"Hi, Katie, this is Tim."

"Oh, Timmy, I'm here with Isabel and Stephanie." There was giggling in the background and both girls called out, "Hi."

Katie continued, "We've been thinking about what happened at the back-to-school party and we feel kinda bad about it. I mean, it wasn't your fault if Emma wanted to talk to you. And you didn't know about her and Jared...."

"And?" I asked. The call was making me feel uncomfortable. Those three girls hadn't said one word directly to me since the party.

"And, we thought that maybe you heard that Stephanie is having a big Halloween party tonight. It's like the most fun party of the year. Everyone dresses up and goes trick-or-treating together and then goes back to the Stiltons for supper and dancing."

"I heard," I answered. How could I not have heard? Everyone in our homeroom had been hearing about the party for ages.

"So we were wondering, would you like to come?"

I had wanted to hear those words all week, but now I hesitated. I didn't really like the kids to begin with, and they had been pretty awful to me. Plus the logistics would be complicated, requiring a taxi there and a pick-up by my parents. I was about to say no, when I realized that Emma would probably be there. Jared would definitely be there and, if he was going, she would, too. After all, it wasn't just Halloween, it was Saturday night. Even if I didn't get to talk Emma, I could watch her dance.

"Yeah, sure," I said.

"You want to come?"

"Yes, I want to come."

There was a pause. "Well, that's too bad, 'cause you're not invited!" There were gales of laughter on the other end. Then, click.

I put the receiver back down. How could I be so stupid? How could I let them set me up like that? Now they knew that I had wanted to be included and that they had gotten to me.

The front doorbell rang. Now what? I turned on the big front hall light and ran downstairs, hoping I'd find some cute little superheroes with their proud parents. I didn't. When I opened the door, no one was there. I was about to slam it shut when I noticed on the stoop a basket surrounded by shaving cream. Inside the basket was an assortment of candy, all in "bite size" wrappers. A note, stuck into the candy, read, "Hey, Bite Size, tonight you can cannibalize."

Whoever had pulled this prank must have been in contact with Stephanie and company. The end of the phone call and the ringing of the doorbell were too well-coordinated to be an accident. Ah, the power of cell phones. I kicked the basket and sent the candy and shaving cream flying. I went back inside, and now I slammed the door.

I hurried through the house to lock the back door, which we always kept unlocked in crime-free Saratoga. I was annoyed that leaving the house open had made me vulnerable. What if the kids who pulled the candy prank had snuck in the back while I was in the front? In case anybody was around, I yelled, "You're all morons!" before running up to my room.

I threw myself down on my bed and thought about how miserable I was in Saratoga. The kids here were stupid, petty, mean, nasty. Soon self-pity turned to self-loathing. I couldn't blame my failure in Saratoga on Saratoga: I had failed everywhere I lived. Why was I such a loser? Why couldn't I ever fit in? I fought back tears and, to distract myself, I grabbed my foam ball and hurled it at the hoop. It totally missed the basket and even the backboard, bouncing off the thick door frame. I got up and retrieved the ball, disgusted with myself. This time, I focused on aiming, but the ball slipped from my fingers at the point of release and bounced, once again, off of the door frame.

"Ok," I said aloud to myself, "this time, it's nothing but net, Ross." I grabbed the ball, and said, in my best sports announcer voice, "Ross has the ball, he's moving up the court. He stops, he shoots, he...misses." My arm had cramped, and the ball hit off the door frame again. I glared at the thick wood as though it were responsible. Then I stopped glaring as I admired how the mahogany stood out about three inches from the wall. The elegant door frames were a theme throughout the house; they were even used on the third floor servants' quarters, where the rooms were smaller and the ceilings lower. You had to hand it to Charles to be willing to spend money on places that would never be seen....

Suddenly, I was moving as fast as I could. I grabbed my flashlight from my desk and the stepstool from my bathroom. With my hands full, I ran up the stairs to the third floor and down the hall to the attic door. I planted the stepstool right in front and climbed up. I couldn't see the top of the door frame, but I could reach it. I put my hand up and ran it slowly over the center of the upper plank. It was covered with dead bugs and decades of dust, but I didn't stop.

I moved my hand to the right, then I strained and felt further back, up against the wall. My fingers touched something cold and hard. I took hold and pulled it forward. It was a key, covered with cobwebs and slightly rusty. I rubbed it on my jeans, switched on my flashlight, and inspected the barrel. Etched in fading letters was the word "Attic."

Chapter Ten

In no time at all, I had climbed off the stool, inserted the key, turned it with a satisfying click, and opened the door. As if the door had been cast in a grade B horror movie, it creaked loudly on its hinges. Inside the door was a narrow, steep staircase, leading to the attic. There was a single bulb fixture at the entry, but when I pulled its string, nothing happened. My flashlight would have to do.

I climbed the stairs carefully, afraid of rotting boards, but I shouldn't have worried. Like everything else in the mansion, the attic access was built solidly. When I reached the top of the stairs, I stepped into the cavernous, high-ceilinged attic. It was illuminated by a little moonlight which filtered through the small inset windows on all four sides. Between the natural light and my flashlight, I could see that the attic was everything I had hoped for. It was a bulging repository of discarded furniture, trunks, open wooden crates of books, and cardboard boxes. I couldn't wait to come back during the day when I could fully explore.

At the center of the back wall stood a wrought iron spiral staircase, disappearing through the top of the roof. Why was there a staircase to the roof? Once again, my knowledge of Victorian houses came in handy. I knew that around the roof's flat top, there was a railed widow's walk. A "widow's walk," on a coastal house, allowed a sailor's wife to look far out to sea for her husband's ship; unfortunately, many a seafaring husband never made it home, which accounts for the tragic name. For Victorians, the widow's walk became a popular feature even on land-locked houses, offering a place to catch the breeze on a hot night.

Since I couldn't explore inside, I decided to climb the spiral staircase. I grabbed a thick book from the top of the pile, then started up. The spiral staircase went past the ceiling of the attic, into a tiny round room. When I stepped onto the room's landing, there was a narrow, low door in front, which was just the right height for me. This door, fortunately, had its key in the lock. I turned the key and pushed the door open. It led out to the large, flat expanse of the roof, surrounded by a delicate white railing that was about knee high.

Once outside, I wedged the book between the door and its frame. The moon's glow allowed me to switch off my flashlight, which I left by the open door. Then I examined the exterior of the round room; it was a miniature of the turret I lived in and served as access to the roof.

The night air was chilly, but windless. Having learned my lesson from that miserable cold in September, I swore I wouldn't stay out long. I began my stroll, being careful not to get too close to the railing. There was a small platform beyond the railing, about twelve inches wide, but it was a long way down if you went over the edge. I headed clockwise from the back turret, along the side of the house toward the front.

Chatsworth Mansion was built on a hill, was three stories tall, and had a high roof. At the top of all that height, the view was amazing. Close by were treetops, and rooftops, and large expanses of grass. Farther off, to the left, were the lights of the town and, to the right, the lights of Skidmore. I wished I had someone to share it all with.

As I advanced from the front to the unexplored side of the widow's walk, I saw that a portion of the railing had been broken and left unrepaired. I had never noticed it from the ground. The top of the railing had splintered and two of the narrow spindles had been cleanly broken off. This must

have been where Chatsworth's son--what was his name?--
had thrown himself to his death. That would explain why I
had found the spectacles in the garden, which lay directly
below. Maybe the broken railing explained even more. I
needed to get a better look and, in my excitement, started
running over.

Just as I arrived at the broken railing, a voice behind me
yelled, "Don't do it!"

I jumped with fright, lost my balance, and teetered on the
edge of the high roof. I felt the terrifying pull of gravity and
fought back. I managed to reach my arms behind me and to
grab the low railing to steady myself. The sickening thought
flitted through my mind that the railing could be rotted and
would give way, causing me to plunge to my death. Fortunately, once again, the excellent Chatsworth construction
held. As soon as I could shift my weight, I moved backwards
on to my butt. I was safe, but not very sound.

I turned to survey the rooftop. Someone had to be there.
Someone who had almost cost me my life. My fury mounted.
This was not an acceptable prank. Shaving cream and
demeaning notes were one thing, endangering a person's life
was another.

I called out, "Who's there?" No one answered.

"Come out, you coward," I said. "Show me your face. I
want a piece of you!" Whoever had scared me was probably
twice my size, but I was hoping that I'd have the advantage
of raging adrenalin.

I yelled again. "You almost killed me, you cretin. Do you
really think that's funny?"

From his hiding place inside the mini-turret, a kid stepped through the open door. He was about my age, maybe a
year or two older. His brown hair was cut short and oiled
back, and he was wearing a Victorian gentleman's costume
with a long black frock coat, fawn pants, a white collared
shirt and a narrow, black bow tie with pointed ends. I had
never seen this kid at the high school, but he was probably

the son of the people giving the writers' party. If I could find out who he was, I would make sure he was punished for stealing into our house, following me up to the roof, and scaring me so badly.

He stepped forward and spoke, in an exaggerated English accent, "I most certainly do not see any humor in the situation. It was not my intention to cause you any harm. On the contrary, I was most eager to assist you. You must promise me that you will never again consider jumping. The fall is terribly painful, I assure you."

"What? You thought I was going to jump?"

"That was the distinct impression you gave me, with your rapid approach to the railing."

This guy was good. On the spot he had come up with a story to cover up his misdeeds. I wasn't going to let him wiggle out of the truth, though.

I said, "I was hurrying over to the railing because I needed a closer look. Then you came along, scared me out of my wits, and almost caused me to fall."

"I am truly sorry about that. You have my sincerest apologies. My only object was to help you."

"If you wanted to help so much," I said disdainfully, "why didn't you just grab hold of me?"

"Unfortunately, I could not."

"Why? Is something wrong with your arms?" There was no indication of any injury.

"No, I just could not...." His voice had become heavy with emotion, as though he might start crying. "I cannot move any physical object."

"And why is that?" I was not letting this guy, with his method acting, off the hook.

He looked dreadfully pained. "I hate to say it. But, if you must know...." He paused, I assumed to try to generate a plausible explanation. His tone changed and became more matter of fact. "Are you a man of honor?"

Will you get a load of this guy? He breaks into my house, follows me around, scares me to within an inch of my death, and then asks me if I'm honorable. Still, I figured I might as well go along for the ride, so I said, "Yes, I am a man of honor, not that it does me much good."

"Then you must swear that you will never tell another soul what I am about to tell you."

"Ok, I swear that your secret will never go beyond this roof."

He took a deep breath and said, "I am a ghost."

I laughed, "Yeah, and I'm a ghoul. Happy Halloween."

He sighed. "This isn't going very well. Let's see. Are you good at fisticuffs?" He assumed a boxing stance, putting his hands up in fists.

"Not at all."

"Just a minute ago you were threatening to hit me."

"The urge has passed. I was angry then, and I still am, but I don't believe in being violent."

"Are you sure that you don't want to hit me now?"

"I'm not the hitting type," I said.

He dropped his fists. "Then will you shake hands?" he asked, sticking out his right hand.

"With the likes of you? No way!"

"Come on, Tim. I would very much like us to be friends."

He knew my name? Of course, he did. Whoever had put him up to this prank had told him my name and address. I had to admit, though, now that I had cooled down a little, I was impressed with the way the kid handled himself. What the hell, I thought, maybe we'll end up friends. Heaven knows, I needed one.

I stood up and put out my hand to shake his, but my hand never made contact. I assumed that he had pulled his hand away quickly in one of those obnoxious moves where the hand-shaker smooths back his hair instead of shaking. It would be just another humiliation for me after so many. But then I looked carefully at his hand and it was still there, outstretched, looking as solid to me as my own hand.

Suddenly, my legs were shaky, and I sank down onto my butt again.

At first, I couldn't seem to find my voice. After a few attempts, I managed to squeak, "You really are a ghost. You're the ghost of Chatsworth Mansion!"

Chapter Eleven

"Yes, I guess technically I am the 'Ghost of Chatsworth Mansion,' although I much prefer to be called by my Christian name: Edmund."

"Of course," I said. "You're Edmund. Charles Chatsworth's younger son. Pleased to meet you." My hand twitched with the urge to shake, but I squelched it.

"I'm pleased to make your acquaintance as well. Tim, I hope you won't think me unduly bold if I suggest that we move our discussion inside, contingent of course on your being capable of walking. It is terribly chilly for you with no overcoat, and I am at a decided disadvantage outdoors."

Going inside to thaw out sounded wonderful to me, if my legs would carry me. I stood up slowly, tested my strength with a few steps, and declared myself ready to descend. Edmund led the way through the open turret door. As I left the roof, I grabbed my flashlight and the book and, after following Edmund down the spiral staircase, I returned the book to the pile.

Edmund offered me a seat on an old dining room chair, but I proposed that we go down to my room, if he was able to leave the confines of the attic. I didn't know what rules a ghost must follow. He explained that, as long as I opened doors for him, he was free to go anywhere in the house. After many years of being trapped in the attic, he was eager to get out.

When we reached the bottom of the attic stairs, I relocked the door, removed the key from the lock, and slipped it into

72

my pants' pocket. That key had given me a lot of trouble, and I wasn't about to let it out of my sight. Then, with stepstool in hand, I led the way down the flight of stairs, through the hall, and into my bedroom.

At the bedroom entrance, Edmund stopped, transfixed. I thought I could see what he was seeing--two twin beds with blue corduroy comforters, a wooden night stand, a blue butterfly chair, a wooden bureau, and a wooden desk with a chair and computer--but maybe I couldn't.

His eyes filled with tears, and he said, "This used to be my bed chamber. My father had it specially designed for me to feel like a lighthouse."

"Why a lighthouse? There aren't exactly ocean views in Saratoga."

"Because I like lighthouses. You see, when I was a lad, I loved to go sailing with my older brother Harold. One time, though, a wonderful excursion turned harrowing when a storm arose, tossing our small boat like a leaf in the wind. We thought all was lost when, suddenly, a light pierced through the dark and rain. We reached the light--which emanated from a lighthouse--and gained entry. The safety and warmth of the lighthouse, after the despair and cold of the storm, never left me. I spoke of it often, and my father, knowing that I was sad to leave my home in England, sought to give me a place of comfort here. And while the room did not afford a lighthouse's observatory, the widow's walk did. This round room was the happiest aspect of my life in America. I'm ever so glad you reside here now, Tim."

I motioned for him to sit down on the butterfly chair, and I propped myself up on the bed. He was clearly an emotional fellow, and I wondered whether he was up to the discussion I had in mind. I hesitated, then decided to try.

"Edmund, I don't mean to pry, but everyone believes that you committed suicide." He looked at me horrified, his already pale demeanor growing paler. I continued, "But you didn't commit suicide, did you?"

Now the tears in his eyes spilled over. "I've been waiting for over a hundred years to hear someone say those words. How did you know?" I was glad that happiness and relief, not sadness and despair, brought out the water-works.

I explained, "Tonight, when I was racing over to the railing, it was not to jump. It was to inspect the damage which suggested a horrible possibility to me. It suggested that a murder had been committed. Someone who wanted to throw himself from the roof would simply step over the low railing onto the outer platform and jump. He wouldn't start his fall from behind the railing. But someone who was standing by the railing, enjoying the view, could be pushed by an attacker from behind. The victim would go flying, his legs and feet breaking through the spindles, and would fall over the edge to his death."

Edmund said, "It's as though you were present that night. You've described exactly what happened. But how could you tell that from just a broken railing? Surely something else could have caused the damage."

"I knew that you had fallen from there because I found these...." I got up and walked over to my bureau, opened my top drawer filled with socks and boxers, and took out the gold spectacles. "They were buried in the garden right below the break."

"My spectacles!" said Edmund, happily. "How proud I was of them. They made me look so distinguished."

I held the frames out, offering them to Edmund. "Oh no," he said. "I'm afraid that, in my current state, I cannot use them." Once again he seemed sad. "I lost so much when I went over the edge." Then, he brightened a bit, "But you gave me back something tonight. At least one person knows the truth and won't think ill of me."

This guy was on an emotional rollercoaster, but I suppose I would be moody, too, if I had been murdered and my murderer had gone unpunished.

To cheer him up I said, "I'll be happy to spread the word. We'll resurrect your reputation and tarnish the murderer's."

Edmund's face darkened again. "But I don't know who murdered me."

"Really?" I asked. Edmund nodded. "Then, we'll just have to figure it out."

"Do you really think we can?"

"It may not be easy, but we'll certainly try." I was already wracking my brain for ways to unravel the crime. Most police detectives consider a case "cold" after a few years. With a case of this vintage, we were talking Antarctica.

Edmund looked pleased. He declared, "If you can help me to solve this mystery, I will be eternally grateful, and I mean that literally."

* * *

Edmund and I talked and talked. We had plenty of time since my parents weren't due back until late. Edmund explained that neither of my parents would see him. Very few people had ever been "seers," and those had all been children. I was by far the oldest seer, and I wasn't yet fifteen. Edmund didn't fully understand the mechanism for breaking the ghost barrier, but it seemed to turn on making an emotional connection. For example, the little girl Rose, the friend of Mr. Henry's mother, had brought flowers to the attic and had danced beautifully and sung sweetly. Edmund had been overjoyed and had shouted, "Bravo!" and the happy child had heard him. His connection with the rotten boy Peter was different, but had the same result. Peter had stormed up to the attic, angry at being alone and bored, and had threatened to destroy all of Edmund's beloved books. Edmund, in turn, was incensed and yelled at Peter, forbidding the destructive act.

I thought about why I saw Edmund. "We must have connected tonight because I was upset that you had been murdered and you were upset that I was going to jump."

Edmund replied, "In truth, we made the connection a good deal earlier. On the day that you tried some keys in the lock and banged on the attic door, we both were terribly frustrated about the missing key. I felt certain that, had the door not been between us, you would have seen me. You could have heard me, too, but I did not speak."

"Didn't you want to cry out for help?"

"I wanted to desperately, but my fear of frightening you kept my mouth closed. I was afraid that if you knew a ghost lived here, you would never come up. But one night--the night after you banged on the door--I could not control myself and called out to you over and over. I did not expect that you would hear me, but it made me feel a bit better."

That explained why hearing my name that night had seemed so real. It had been.

I asked, "Why didn't you present yourself to me tonight as soon as I came up?"

"I've never connected with someone close to my own age, and I didn't know how you would respond. I wasn't sure if I would ever reveal myself to you, but I certainly wasn't going to do it in the dark of night. However, when I thought you were going to jump, I had to speak."

"One thing I don't understand," I said, "is why you made me swear to keep your secret. I will do it, of course, but if nobody can see you, nobody can harm you."

"I made you promise, not for my safety, but for your own. Nothing good has ever come from a seer telling others of my existence. Unless you relish spending time in an asylum, it's best not to say anything to anyone."

"It's true that most people wouldn't believe me."

"'There are more things in Heaven and Earth than are dreamt of in your philosophy,'" said Edmund.

"I've heard that before. It's Shakespeare, right?"

"Right. Hamlet says it after seeing his father's ghost. It means that things may exist that cannot be rationally explained. But to be perfectly honest, until I myself became a ghost, I did not believe in ghosts. Even now, I find it difficult to believe."

"Yeah, well that makes two of us." I kept pinching my arms to make sure I was awake. I'd probably have bruises in the morning. "I'd love to understand more about your life as a ghost; that is, if you feel comfortable talking about it."

"I'm happy to share what I know with you, but I must warn you, I am woefully unknowledgeable about ghostly matters outside of my own, limited experience. I am not acquainted with other ghosts with whom I can compare notes. That being said, I will happily answer your questions as best I can. What would you like to know?"

"Well, for starters, you used to wear spectacles, but you said you can't anymore. Do you see well without them?"

"One advantage to being a ghost is that vision correction is not necessary. My vision, hearing and sense of smell all are excellent, perhaps to compensate for my lack of taste and touch."

"You can't feel or taste anything?"

"A ghost cannot touch physical objects nor can he eat."

I thought, Katie would love this guy's diet. All smelling, no eating.

I said, "I noticed that you walk around and climb stairs. Can't ghosts fly?"

"I don't believe I can, but I must admit I've never tried. Old habits die hard. I like having the exercise, and I like the familiar feel of moving my legs. Moving this way makes me feel more...normal."

"And why, if you look so solid to me, did my hand pass right through you?"

"I seem to be made of air, yet give the illusion of solidity to seers. By the way, all the stories of being able to pass through walls are nonsense. Can air pass through walls? No. Thank goodness that tonight you propped open the turret door. If you hadn't, I would have remained shut inside and we wouldn't be talking now."

"And you might never have spoken to me. You might have stayed locked up forever."

"That's a dreadful thought. I have been confined for ever-so long. The parents of the bad boy, Peter, locked the door to keep their son out, not to keep me in. Since then, few people have ventured up. The last were the dreadful couple who tried to make the house a freakish curiosity."

"Did you ever have a chance to escape?"

"For a brief period, when the innkeepers were removing attic furniture to use in the rooms, I could have moved downstairs. But I decided that being alone in the attic was preferable to being unseen down below. You have no idea how painful it is to watch others' lives unfolding while being unseen and ignored yourself."

Actually, I had a really good idea of how it felt, but my eight or so years of discomfort seemed dwarfed in comparison to Edmund's long trial.

"I just thought of something: if you never came downstairs, how did you know my name?"

"Whenever I hear people coming near the attic door, I hurry down the stairs to listen. On the day you arrived, I thought your name was 'Tommy' because that's what the shrill woman called you, but when you came back to test the keys, you called yourself 'Tim.' I corrected what I called you in my thoughts. At the risk of sounding foolish, I paid special attention to your presence from the outset because I had a feeling that you would be important to me."

"It doesn't sound foolish. I had an irrational obsession with getting into the attic. I spent weeks and weeks looking for the key. I didn't know why I had to find it, but I knew I had to."

"Where did you finally find the key?"

"On top of the attic door frame."

"So near, and yet so far. Well, thank heavens you found it. The last twenty-five years have been unbearably dull. I felt I was going mad with the tedium."

78

I often felt that way after a particularly boring math class. I definitely needed an attitude adjustment. Trying to find a happier topic, I said, "There must be things you do to keep busy. Tell me how you spend your days."

"Mostly I daydream. I like to think of happy times before my brother's accident. Oh, and I try to move around a lot. Exercise is very important to good health, you know."

I did know, although I wasn't sure how that applied to the ghost world. "You have lots of books up there. Do you like to read?"

Edmund sighed. "I *love* to read, or I should say, I *loved* to read. But I'm afraid I'm a modern day Tantalus. You do remember that myth, don't you?"

"Not exactly." Greek myths weren't detective stories.

"Well, I shall remind you. Tantalus, the son of Zeus, was invited to eat with the gods. Unwisely, he misbehaved and was punished with excruciating thirst and hunger. Immersed up to his neck in water, he would bend to drink, only to find the water had drained away. Surrounded by trees bearing luscious fruits, he would reach up to pluck one, only to find the wind had blown away the branches. I am like Tantalus. My books lay in front of me, ready to inform and entertain, but I lacked the ability to pick them up or turn their pages."

"Maybe you could learn to move objects. There are lots of stories of ghosts making noise, especially at night."

"Those noises are probably just the wind or mice. Or perhaps some ghosts have different powers and mine are sadly limited." This seemed to be a new, distressing thought. "Do you think other ghosts really can move objects? Do you think other ghosts can move through walls? Do you think that I am just an unaccomplished ghost?"

His voice quavered. I decided that it was time to change the subject. There was a murder to be solved and, like Saratoga in mid-autumn, it was just getting colder and colder with each passing moment.

Chapter Twelve

"The first thing we need to do," I said to Edmund, "is to generate a list of likely suspects." I had gotten up off my bed and was pacing back and forth between the bed and the door. For fun, I had donned my deerstalker cap, a present from my Grandpa Cohen, and was holding a calabash pipe, a present from my Grandpa Ross. Maybe I should have felt silly, but I had never had a client who looked like he belonged in a Sherlock Holmes mystery. Actually, I could have ended that sentence after "I had never had a client," but I liked the excuse to don a costume.

I asked, "Did you have a butler?"

"Yes, of course we did."

"He might have done it. Butlers are often guilty of crimes."

Edmund shook his head. "It is highly unlikely that Hobson did it. All the servants were out that night, my father having given them leave to go to the county fair. Early that evening, I watched all fourteen of them, dressed in their Sunday attire, head down the long driveway and into town. I suppose one of them could have returned surreptitiously to the house."

"It's possible, but unlikely. Let's first consider the people who you know were in the house."

"There were only three people, other than myself, in the house that night."

"And they were...." I put down the pipe on my desk and took up a small notebook and pencil.

"They were my father, my stepmother Hattie, and my stepbrother Albert."

I wrote down the names as a list and asked, "And how would you rank those three as to likelihood of guilt?"

Edmund paused to think. "My father is the easiest case. I would stake my life on his innocence." I didn't point out the impossibility of this statement. Edmund added emphatically, "He did not murder me."

"You're probably right, but we can't rule him out just yet." I put a number "3" next to Charles's name in my notebook. "Who would you put as the next least likely?"

"I suppose Albert. I didn't particularly like him, but I didn't dislike him either. We just had very little to do with one another. He was a few years older than I, and he was always off with attractive young ladies at theatrical events or horse races or dinners."

I wrote a "2" next to Albert's name. "And I assume that you would rank your stepmother as the most likely suspect." I put a "1" next to Hattie's name.

"Yes, I would. She was a horrible woman, a money-hungry harridan. Before she wed my father, she was all sweetness and kindness. She doted on him and almost as much on me. But the ink on the wedding certificate was scarcely dry before she made her true character known. She was interested in my father only for his money and his position, but at least she was interested. Since I had neither, she had no use for me. Had she left me alone, I could have endured her presence. But she harped on my 'entrenched, depraved nature' and tried to turn my father against me. She found fault in everything I did. If I studied hard, she accused me of familial neglect. If I turned my attention to my family, she accused me of academic laziness. When I urged my father to leave Saratoga and return to England with me, she said I was selfish for denying him the curative waters. And when I asked to return alone, she said I was selfish for denying my father my company."

81

"I'm surprised that she didn't urge you to return to England."

"I think she was afraid that, if I left, so would my father. But even if he had stayed, he probably wouldn't have lasted long without me. In that regard, Hattie was right. She wanted him to stay alive because, while he was alive, she could spend his money. Once he died, she was entitled only to her widow's share; the rest of the estate would go to me."

I was scribbling notes furiously during the Hattie discussion. She did seem the most likely candidate, based on motive and character.

I said, "You've done an excellent job of assessing the situation. Here's what I propose: we begin our investigation with the least likely candidate so we can quickly rule out extraneous leads, and then we'll move up the ladder."

"I don't mean to question your methodology, but doesn't that seem a bit inefficient?"

"Not really. While we're working on each candidate, we'll uncover important clues."

"Well, I have placed myself in your capable hands. You discovered the mystery of my murder and now I am confident that you will solve it. But I still don't believe my father could be guilty."

"Perhaps his true character was not entirely known to you. Would you have expected him to marry a woman like Hattie? Or, having married her, would you expect him to stay with her? Perhaps he felt that Hattie's dislike for you was an impediment to his happiness. Or perhaps you were too painful a reminder of his grave loss."

"All that is possible, but improbable."

"Often, writers put their unconscious thoughts into their work. Did your father ever include murder scenes in his books?"

At this question, Edmund's eyes grew large. "He did. His dramatic murder scenes were a key element of his public appeal. In almost all his books, he included a low-life character who committed murders without compunction."

"Now we're cooking with gas," I said. Edmund looked at me funny. I explained, "Oh, that's just an expression. It means, 'now we're getting somewhere.'"

"You'll definitely think we've gotten somewhere when I tell you that one of my father's books, the one that he wrote while we were living here, includes a murder scene where the hero is lured to the roof of a large house and is pushed off the widow's walk."

"That's incredible!"

Edmund's voice shook as he said, "To think of it would make my blood run cold, if I still had blood." Once again, Edmund's eyes welled with tears.

I tried to distract him. "Do you remember the details of the scene? I'm sure it would be helpful."

Edmund paused, collecting himself. "I'm afraid I have only a vague recollection. I haven't thought of the book--it's called *A Fall From Grace*--for a very long time. But the written word is immortal. All we have to do is get a copy, and we can read it together."

"I'll run up to the attic and get it now."

"That would be a capital idea, if I owned the book. Unfortunately, none of the books in the boxes is by my father. The books in the attic were my school books, and my father's works were not taught at Eton."

"Then we'll have to find a copy elsewhere." I yawned and noticed that the clock on the nightstand said 11:25. "Tomorrow morning, I'll see if my mother has it. But now, we should go to sleep. That is, I should. Do you sleep?"

Edmund responded, "I do. Old habits die hard." He looked rather glum. "Well, I'd better head back up to the attic. Would you mind bringing me up there to open the door? I suppose, if you're too tired, I could sleep in one of the unoccupied bedrooms."

I got the hint. "Listen, Edmund, my parents will probably check on me to make sure I'm asleep, but nobody will be using the other bed. If you want to sleep there, you're welcome to. After all, it's your room as much as mine. Actually, it's more yours, since it was built for you."

Edmund smiled. "If you really don't mind, I would enjoy a night's repose in the old bed chamber. I can't thank you enough for your generous offer."

"It's my pleasure. I'm just going to get ready for bed and then it will be lights out." I was excited about having a sleep over. When I had first moved into my bedroom, I had asked my mother to remove the extra bed, but she had put me off, saying it might come in handy. Since I have no siblings or cousins to use it, she must have been hoping I'd have a friend who would. Now I did, sort of.

I rushed through brushing my teeth, washing my face, and changing into pajamas. Back in the room, Edmund had moved from the butterfly chair to the extra bed. He was lying on it, but didn't make any indentation on the bed or pillow. It looked weird, especially since he was fully and formally attired.

I turned off the overhead light, climbed into bed, and turned off the table lamp.

"Good night, Edmund, I wish you pleasant dreams."

"Good night, Tim. I hope that tomorrow we will be cooking with very much gas."

* * *

The smell of bacon, scrambled eggs, and toasted bagel teased my nose. I opened my eyes to see my father standing over me with a plateful of steaming food and a glass of orange juice. Neither of my parents were cooks, but a simple breakfast was within my dad's abilities. He must have been feeling mighty guilty about something to bring me breakfast in bed.

"Hey, Timmy Tiger, it's time to rise and shine. You sure slept late. It's almost nine o'clock."

The fog of sleepiness was starting to lift. I had slept soundly, better than I had in weeks. For the first time since we had moved in, I hadn't stayed up late, thinking of places to search for the key. I had found the key and...Edmund. I sat up abruptly and looked over at the other bed. Edmund was sitting up, grinning broadly and deeply inhaling the breakfast-scented air. To remind me to be discreet, he put a finger up to his lips.

"Gee, Dad, that plate of food sure smells great. If I hadn't eaten for about a hundred and twenty-five years, this would be the perfect meal for me to smell."

"Thanks, Timmy, for the unusual, yet gratifying compliment." He passed me the plate, and I dug in. I was relieved that Edmund couldn't eat; otherwise, I would have felt really guilty.

After a few bites, I asked, "And to what do I owe the pleasure of this fine repast?"

"Can't I just make my number one son a hearty breakfast without raising eyebrows?"

Mine were raised and so were Edmund's.

"Nope, Dad. I'm afraid you're as transparent as a ghost." Edmund laughed. "So why don't you just tell me what's up?"

"Well, it's such a beautiful autumn day that your mother and I agreed to have all your grandparents visit. They've been asking to come since we first moved in. They really want to see the house and, of course, you. They'll only stay for lunch and dinner, though, not overnight."

"They'll be here for lunch? That's in only three hours."

"Actually, they'll be here in about two hours. They got an early start."

"Geez, Dad, I wish you had asked me first. I have a lot to do today." Which was true, although I had already finished all my homework. What I had to do was track down a copy of *A Fall From Grace* and read the pertinent chapter to Edmund.

"You're probably right that I should have asked you. It's just that your grandparents have something important to discuss with you. But I promise that next time I'll check with you first. So, how about you get going? I bet you can get everything done before they get here."

"Good idea." I put the last of the eggs on top of the last of the bagel and popped it in my mouth. "Thanks for the bribe, Dad. It was delicious...and very odiferous, in a totally good way." I handed him the plate and headed to the door. "By the way," I asked, "how was last night?"

"Splendid! We had a jolly good time." This last sentence he said in a British accent, a tribute to his brief stint as Charles Dickens. Then he must have remembered that I had spent the night alone. "That is to say, it was quite pleasant for a bunch of unnecessary nonsense. We met some nice people. Was your evening tolerable?" He looked at me hopefully.

"I can say, without hesitation, that it was one of the best evenings in recent memory." And by "recent memory" I meant the last fourteen and a half years of my life.

"Did anything special happen?" Dad asked.

"Nothing to speak of." Which was also true, since I had sworn to Edmund to keep his secret.

"I'm very glad you enjoyed yourself. It's a gift to be able to make your own good time." My dad picked up my foam ball in his free hand and took an easy shot. He missed, and the ball bounced off the door frame.

Chapter Thirteen

After I took a shower and threw on some grubby Sunday clothes, I brought Edmund downstairs with me to look for my mother. As he surveyed the passing rooms, Edmund's gaze was intense. The house must have been a shadow of its former glory, but Edmund seemed happy to see it again.

We found my mother alone in the library, taking notes from a big, fat novel. Her work was spread out on one side of the enormous desk; my father's work was on the other. They enjoyed sharing the vast work space and, when both were in the room, pretended to communicate via semaphore.

As I entered, my mom looked up from her book. "Hi, dear, did you enjoy breakfast?"

"I did. Although I'm not sure how much I'll enjoy lunch and dinner."

"I know, Tim, I know. But think how much you mean to your grandparents."

Actually, that was the problem in a nutshell. If I meant a little less, I'd have more breathing space. It wasn't easy being the only grandchild of four intense people.

I changed the subject. "Mom, I was wondering if the world's foremost collection of Victorian novels..." here, I gestured to the shelves of books she had unpacked, "...contains a copy of *A Fall From Grace.*"

"That's Chatsworth, isn't it?"

"So I hear."

"If I have it, it would be on that shelf," she pointed near the top, "...where the Cs are. But I don't think I've ever read it, hence I don't think I own it. You know that I, and the rest of the world, find Chatsworth melodramatic and verbose."

Edmund's face grew red, and he clenched his fists and blinked his eyes. Precipitation couldn't be far behind.

"Now, Mom, I'm sure Chatsworth still has his fans."

"I doubt it," she said, oblivious to the pain she was inflicting.

"But you said that he was very well-liked in his day. Maybe he wrote melodrama because it appealed to his audience, not because it was his natural style."

"Perhaps. The only way to discover whether his style got corrupted would be to compare his early, unknown works to his later popular ones. Nobody reads his early works nowadays; if anything is read, it's his two last novels."

Edmund looked a little calmer; the bright red in his face was now a pale pink and his hands were relaxed.

"If I wanted to find a copy of *A Fall From Grace*, where would I go?"

"Have you tried the Internet?"

I already had, before I came downstairs. I had found only one copy listed. It was expensive because it was "rare," and it was all the way in Australia. It would take forever to get here. "Yeah, I checked. It wasn't a great option. Any other ideas?"

"You could start with the library since this is Chatsworth country. Or, you could try the used bookstore on Phila Street. I don't remember its name."

"Good idea, Mom. Thanks. I'm going to head out now, but I'll be back in time for the invasion."

Edmund and I went back up to our room to get my wallet with my library card and money.

Once the door was closed, Edmund asked, "Why was your mother criticizing my father's work? Doesn't she know he's one of the greatest writers in the English language? He's in the pantheon with Shakespeare, Milton, and Chaucer."

Not wanting my parents to hear me "talking to myself," I whispered as I explained to Edmund that today's beloved "classic" is often tomorrow's doorstop. That literary tastes change and only a small handful of books ever transcend time and place. Edmund was looking glum again.

On the other hand, I offered, if his father's work had gone out of fashion, perhaps it could be brought back into fashion. Edmund looked more cheerful and said that, in addition to solving his murder mystery, we must restore his father's reputation. I had a feeling I would be too busy to play indoor basketball for a long time.

* * *

As I was leaving the house to get my bike, my dad called out from the kitchen, "Don't forget to be back by eleven. Your grandparents won't want to miss a moment of your company."

"Don't worry, Dad. I'll be back at eleven...pm."

"Very funny. And while you're in town, can you pick up a couple of the Putnam Market muffins? I want to serve them with tea,but I forgot to buy them." Two of their gigantic muffins would be enough for all seven of us to share.

Although I had invited Edmund to join me, I was traveling solo. He had more fully explained, what he had alluded to the night before, that he didn't do well outside because a strong gust of wind could carry him off. Katie's big backpack had inspired me to propose using my equally big backpack to carry Edmund in, but he had declined the offer. I think he just wanted some time alone in his old room.

My first stop was the library. In the computer catalog, I found Chatsworth's book, but it wasn't on the shelf. When I asked the librarian, she explained that the book had not been checked out since 1952 and was in storage. Unfortunately, since it was Sunday, they had no access to storage, and I probably couldn't get the book until mid-week.

I hopped on my bike and rode the short distance to the used bookstore which, I discovered, was called Twice Told

Books. Ten o'clock was early for a Sunday opening, but there was a light on. I peered through the glass door and saw a white-haired woman taking down books, swiping at them with an old-fashioned feather duster, and placing them back on the shelf. I rapped lightly on the door. She looked up from her work and scurried over.

Pointing to the front window, she barked, "Can't you read the sign? We don't open till twelve."

"I didn't see it. Sorry. I'll come back later...tomorrow." It killed me that she wouldn't let me in, but as my dad always says: if you don't have a choice, you don't have a problem.

She said, "Well, if you're going to be that way about it, I guess you can come in."

I wasn't sure what she meant, but the door was open, and I was on a mission. Once I was inside, she asked, "What is it you're looking for?"

"A book..." I started to say.

I was going to continue, named *A Fall From Grace*, but she interrupted me, "I could have guessed that. You wouldn't come to this shop for a hat or a Parcheesi board."

I said politely, "A particular book named *A Fall From Grace* by...."

She interrupted me again, "Charles Chatsworth. Yup, I've got that one. Got a whole bunch of Chatsworth."

"You do?" I was trying not to sound too excited.

"Haven't had anyone request that book for, oh, about a hundred years." She paused, "Got you, didn't I? You were thinking I've been around for a hundred years, but it just feels that way sometimes."

Was this a segue into her life story which would be long, albeit shorter than a hundred years' worth? I thought I'd nip it in the bud. "I don't mean to be rude, but I'm in a bit of a hurry."

"Everybody's always in a hurry these days. They rush from their computer screens at home to their computer screens at work. The fine art of conversation is a thing of the past. Oh well, follow me."

She headed through a passage off the front room, into a warren of small rooms and passageways. At the very back, we entered a room filled with finely bound volumes. These books were beautiful, with leather bindings of many colors and gilt work. They came from an age when the book itself, not just its contents, was precious.

The old woman pointed to a set on a high shelf. "That's the Chatsworth."

I quickly counted fourteen volumes. She motioned to a stepstool, and I climbed up to get *A Fall From Grace*. It was magnificent, with dark green leather covering the front and back covers. There was a leafy design cut into the leather and gilded. Unfortunately, it would cost a fortune.

"Tell me," she said, "What do you want with the Chatsworth?"

I told her as much as I could. "I'm doing some research on him. My parents and I live in the old mansion, so I've gotten kind of interested."

"Hmm. I had a fancy decorator in the other day. She spotted that set and said she had to have it. Offered me a bundle for it, too. Guess what she was going to do with it?"

"Put it in somebody's library?"

"Right. But not to read. Just to take up shelf space. She buys books by the foot to make 'shelves look pretty.' Can you imagine, buying books to use as decoration? I know people don't read Chatsworth a lot these days. All they want are books like *He's Just Not That Into You*—well, of course, he isn't, if you're silly enough to read a book like that. If people read the good stuff, like Austen and Dickens, they'd learn a thing or two about life and love. Anyway, you wouldn't buy the set just to make your shelves look pretty, would you?"

I actually thought they would look nice in the library, but I was planning to read at least part of *A Fall From Grace*. Maybe I could interest Mom in taking a look. And Edmund would be overjoyed to have the set around. "I can't promise that they'll all be read, but at least some parts will be."

"That's good enough for me. These old men need a good home, and Chatsworth Mansion seems like just the place. How about I charge you ten dollars a volume? That would be…" she scanned the shelf, counting, "…one hundred and forty dollars."

I knew it was an incredible bargain. The single, plain copy on the Internet had been half that amount. I had some birthday money sitting in my bank account. This seemed like a good way to spend it.

"Sure. That sounds very reasonable."

She said, "Well, if you're going to be that way about it, how about five dollars a volume?"

The old woman was cracked, but in a good way.

"That would be ok with me, if it suits you," I said.

"You drive a hard bargain. But everyone comes out ahead. You get the books you need, the books get the home they need, and I get the shelf space I need."

"I'm afraid I can't give you the shelf space yet. I came on my bike. If you don't mind, I'll take this volume with me, and I'll send over my dad tomorrow for the rest."

"That'll be just fine. Let's go settle up."

I followed her through the maze to the front. She wasn't kidding when she said she needed shelf space; books were crammed into shelves and stacked all over the floor. At the register I gave her a twenty dollar deposit and she gave me a receipt.

I headed to the door, but stopped before leaving, and said, "Thank you very much for sharing your books with me. I promise to treasure them always."

She picked up her feather duster and acted busy. "Get along with you. Now you really are in a hurry. You've got a new book to read.

Chapter Eighteen

"I got it!" I told Edmund, holding out the book to show him. As soon as I had walked in the house, I had dumped the muffins in the kitchen and raced up to my room. Edmund had been sitting on his bed, watching time pass on the digital clock.

When he saw the book, Edmund said, "Good show, Tim. What a beauty it is. Can we read it?"

I checked the clock myself. We had about twenty minutes until arrival. "Sure. We can at least get started." Before I opened the book, though, I pulled a dirty tee-shirt out of my closet hamper and wiped the book's cover carefully. The bookstore's feather duster probably hadn't touched the Chatsworth volumes in years. Then I opened the pages, with their crisp, gilded edges.

"How far back do you think the chapter is?" I asked.

"Quite a ways. Maybe the penultimate chapter, or the one before that. I suggest you consult the table of contents. My father's books always had descriptive chapter headings."

I turned to the table of contents, skimmed down it and found the heading near the end of the list.

"Here it is!" I read aloud, "'Wherein a good man is sent to meet his maker and, unwittingly, gets his revenge.' Bingo."

"What is 'Bingo'?"

"Oh, it's an expression that comes from a game of chance. It means, I've found exactly what I was looking for."

93

I turned to the back of the book, thumbing through until I found the right page. "Let's begin," I said, then I cleared my throat and read:

Edgar stepped out from the little turret house onto the expanse of the flat roof, which was fenced in with a delicate white railing that shone like lace against the darkening sky. It had been a sunny day, warm and gentle, but now gray clouds were gathering and the autumn wind began to blow. Edgar removed a well-worn sheaf of paper from inside his frock coat breast pocket. He had chosen this pocket for the paper's lodging, not because of its safety and easy access, but because the penned sentiments would be close to his heart. In the rapidly fading light, Edgar read the note, written in the hand he loved so dearly, although he already knew the words by heart.

My dearest Edgar, Meet me upon the rooftop on Tuesday at 6pm. I wouldst have a word with you about our secret plans for matrimony. Until then, I remain your loving,

Little Angelina.

Ah, how aptly she was named, thought Edgar. The angels themselves had not sweeter dispositions nor lovelier aspects. How he hated to set her at odds against her good father by engaging her in a clandestine promise of marriage. Such subterfuge was doubly loathsome as he had been treated with kindness by the old man ever since he had come to the Wixsted house as a young orphan, eager to study the law. Now Edgar was a lawyer, with excellent prospects for the future, but not sufficiently established to take on the responsibilities of a wife.

Edgar heard the handle of the turret door turning and his heart pounded with anticipation and love. Soon his beloved girl would step lightly across the rooftop and be by his side, whispering her darling nonsense in his ear. Yet when the door opened, it was not Angelina who emerged, but the horrible clerk Orrick, carrying a glowing lantern in his ink-stained fingers. He left the door open as if he planned to leave quickly.

"Fancy meeting you up here, Master Edgar," said Orrick. "You wouldn't be planning to meet someone, now would you?"

"That is none of your affair, Orrick. I would beg you leave this place, as it is already occupied."

"But I am in no hurry, and there is plenty of room here for two...or three."

"If you will not leave, then I shall." Edgar hated to vacate the place, thereby forfeiting a chance to be with his winsome girl, but he had no choice.

As Edgar strode across the roof towards the open door, Orrick, who was bigger and stronger, blocked his way.

"What mean you, sir, by this impertinence?" Edgar demanded.

"I mean to have a word with you. But first I must take this..." Orrick snatched the sheaf of paper from Edgar's hand, then stuck its corner into the flame through the top of the lantern. The tiny flame spread until it engulfed the entire sheaf.

"No!" cried Edgar

"Do not fret so, Master Edgar. It was not the precious document you think, although I must admit it was quite precious to me. You see, that note was the finest example of my exquisite copying abilities. Or, should I say, the second finest example?"

"What mean you, sir?   You are talking nonsense."

"The note I have here," Orrick paused to pat the breast pocket of his coat, "Is also in the hand of Miss Angelina, as counterfeited by yours truly. In it, the girl tells you that, although she loves you, she can never marry you. She could never defy the wishes of her beloved father to satisfy your desires."

"Angelina would never say that. What fiendish purpose do you have in creating these falsehoods?"

"My purpose is to give the world an explanation for your suicide."

"My what?"

"Your terrible jump from this rooftop. You will fall, and then I shall run back downstairs to my desk where I am copying letters for Mr. Wixsted. When the police arrive on the rooftop, they shall find the letter from Angelina anchored by the lantern."

"You are mad, Orrick!"

"Just mad in love. I must have Angelina as my own. Whilst you live, she has no eyes for me. But once you are gone, her eyes will be opened."

"She will deny that she wrote this forgery. You will be found out."

"I think not. She may deny it, but all will believe that she is just shrinking from the responsibility of your demise. She will be shunned for her cruelty in rejecting you, but I will not shun her. I alone will stand by her."

"You shall never have her. Never!"

Orrick laughed diabolically and lunged at Edgar. The two men wrestled, each straining with all his might, knowing the stakes were of the highest order. In time, however, Edgar proved no match against the larger Orrick. With a final great effort, the fiend pushed the good man over the edge of the roof. Edgar screamed as he fell, and then there was a thud and silence.

Calmly, as if nothing had occurred, Orrick removed the forged letter from his breast pocket and placed a corner of it under his lantern. It was a good thing the letter was anchored for suddenly a great gust of wind swept over the roof. The door to the turret slammed shut.

Orrick moved to the door, eager to make his descent, but when he took hold of the handle to turn it, it remained stationary in his hand. He pulled on it forcefully, to no avail. The door was locked. He tried to kick in the door, but even his powerful legs had no effect on the solid, thick wood. Down below on the ground, he heard a great commotion as people gathered to view the fallen Edgar. Orrick thought to call out, but he was loath to reveal himself at the scene of the crime just yet. He would have to tell the police a story when they came barging through. Perhaps he would say that he had heard the commotion, had run up to check for a suicide note, and had found Angelina's note instead. Then he could say that the door slammed shut and trapped him.

In just two more minutes, he could shout out to the crowd below. But when the two minutes had passed, the crowd had dispersed and there was no one to shout to. He waited on the cold, blustery roof through the night, and when the police finally arrived in the morning, they found Orrick, clutching in his hands a strip of paper with the name Angelina upon it, having frozen to his death.

Having finished the chapter, I shut the book.

"Bravo, Tim," said Edmund, clapping his hands. "Well read!"

"Do you really think so?" I hadn't been trying to do anything special, although I had gotten caught up in the action and had used different voices for the two males.

"I know so. The last time I enjoyed a reading so much was when I was little and my father took me to hear Charles Dickens read from *The Mystery of Edwin Drood*. You may not know this, but Mr. Dickens was almost as great a theatrical performer as he was a writer."

"Well, thanks for the compliment. Next time I'll put a hat out and collect tips."

"I shall be sure to have suitable coins and flowers to throw at you. But tell me, did you learn anything about my father from reading the chapter?"

"I learned he had a strong sense of right and wrong which makes it less likely that he was a murderer. He certainly believed in punishing evil, although I'm surprised that he let Orrick send poor Edgar overboard to his death."

"Oh, Edgar went overboard, but he didn't die."

"Of course he died. He fell three or four stories. Nobody survives that." I had proof positive of this assertion standing right in front of me, but it seemed impolite to point that out.

"Maybe not in real life, but in a novel he does. Now that I've heard the chapter, I remember the details of the ending clearly. Shall I tell you what happens or would you prefer to read it?"

"Tell me."

"To the best of my recollection, Edgar falls, but lands in a large pile of leaves and, although he is injured, survives. Angelina nurses him back to health and, while he is convalescing, her father realizes how invaluable the young lawyer is to the practice. Wixsted makes Edgar a full partner and, now, can have no objections to the marriage."

"So, the good are rewarded and the bad are punished."

"Even more than you know, for the attempted murder becomes a big news story, carried in all the British papers. Edgar is described in the stories not only by name, but by his physical appearance which includes an unusual mushroom-shaped mark on his cheek. Reading the story is Edgar's long-lost uncle who is the enormously wealthy, childless Duke of Avon. He knows Edgar by the distinguishing mark and begs him to come live at the ancestral home. Edgar agrees, as long as he is free to wed Angelina and make her a Duchess."

"And they all live happily and richly ever after," I said.

Edmund replied, "Isn't that the way all books are supposed to end?"

I didn't want to hurt Edmund's feelings, but books no longer had to end that way unless they were Harlequin Romances. I could see why this book didn't appeal to modern readers. It was like Charles Dickens on steroids. All the elements of coincidence and retribution were so magnified as to be preposterous. On the other hand, I had been pretty riveted to the narrative. There was a polish and vigor to Chatsworth's writing.

"I noticed the hero's name was Edgar. Any chance that was in your honor?" I asked.

"After I was born, my father gave many of his heroes names similar to mine. Besides Edgar, there is an Edwin, an Edward, an Edsel, and an Edwald."

"My mother is a big believer in the relevance of name choice in authors' works. If your father chose to name his good guys after you, he probably thought of you as a good guy."

"Then you don't think that my father was my murderer?"

"Before I answer that question, let me ask you one: who in this household would have read this book when it was published?"

"Everyone."

"Including your stepmother and stepbrother?"

"Not just including them, especially them. They and I read my father's work while it was still in manuscript form, then in the serials, and later when published. My father was meticulous about catching spelling and printing errors, and we all assisted him in proof-reading."

"It's very possible that, while your father wrote about a rooftop murder staged to look like a suicide, someone else borrowed his idea for real life. Your father appears as innocent as you say. I just wish we had absolute proof. Something more tangible and personal."

"Like what?"

"Well, the most telling evidence would be a diary, but in its absence I would take a calendar."

Edmund said, "Then we must go immediately to my father's desk!"

I hated to burst his bubble. "If there was something there before, it isn't there now. I checked every inch of the desk when I was looking for the key."

"But did you discover the false bottom on the lowest right-hand drawer?"

Now I was excited. "There's a false bottom?! Is there a diary in there?"

"Bingo," he said.

Chapter Fifteen

"Will you look at this gorgeous boy?! No, not boy. Young man. What are you waiting for, Mr. Gorgeous? Do you think it's everyday that your Grandma Deena gets kisses from a handsome, young man?"

Grandma Deena grabbed me and, before I could protect myself, covered my face with wet kisses and, for her grand finale, pinched my cheeks. My grandparents had arrived in all their larger-than-life glory, and my parents and I had rushed outside to greet them.

"Hello, Tim dear," said my Grandma Sondra who had been waiting patiently to greet me. She gave me a hug and a kiss, then stepped back. "You look wonderful, dear. I think you've grown quite a bit. Really, I do."

"Nah. He hasn't grown," said my Grandpa Donald, handing me a pair of loafers. "He's way too short for his age." Turning to my mother, he said, "Get him to an endocrinologist, Susan, pronto. At this rate, he'll be lucky to reach five two and then where will he be? He won't get a job and he won't get a girl."

"He'll always be a mental giant, and that's what really counts," said my Grandpa Sam, handing me a bowler hat. "Don't you worry, Tim. Napoleon was short, and he conquered the world. So will you."

Grandma Sondra piped up, "And don't forget, Don, that your David didn't grow until late. He must have been at least eighteen or nineteen before he finished his growth. I'm sure

Tim will grow to be just right." She smiled encouragingly at me.

My dad, hoping to end the discussion on this positive note, interrupted, "Now that you've had a chance to scrutinize Tim, how about you come inside and scrutinize our new house?"

Before the onslaught, I had explained to Edmund that it's easy to remember who's who in our family because, on my dad's side, everyone has a "D" name: Donald, Deena, and David. On my mom's side, everyone has an "S" name: Sam, Sondra, and Susan. When my mom was pregnant with me and the sonogram revealed I was a boy, the Rosses loudly lobbied for me to be named Dean, or Dylan, or Dexter. The Cohens quietly lobbied for Scott, or Steven, or Stuart. My parents diplomatically named me Timothy.

Besides the letter-coded names, my grandparents are easily distinguishable because they are well-matched sets. My Cohen grandparents are sweet, and kind, and agree on everything. My Ross grandparents are feisty, and hyper-critical (Grandpa Don) or hyper-flattering (Grandma Deena), and agree on nothing. I would have happily spent lots of time with my Cohen grandparents, but the problem is, the two couples are inseparable. When they gave up their next-door houses, they moved into next-door apartments. I have never understood how such different people came to be friends, but they have a long history binding them together and, of course, now they have me.

My grandfathers had even owned similar businesses. Grandpa Sam had been in hats and Grandpa Don had been in shoes. As they liked to say, they could take care of me "from head to toe." Unfortunately, hats had gone from being an absolute necessity in the first half of the twentieth century to being a novelty item. Unlike hats, shoes remained a necessity, but imports from Asia had captured a large share of the market. Both grandfathers had gone from being reasonably wealthy to being only modestly so. Both were now retired, but they still had friends in their industries, which explains their unusual gifts to me.

Wearing my new bowler hat and loafers, I led everyone on a full tour of the house except, of course, for the attic. Grandma Deena gushed about everything from the hardwood floors to the coffered ceilings. Grandpa Don criticized everything from the excessive number of stairs to the excessive number of rooms. My Cohen grandparents just smiled and said they were sure we'd be very happy there.

Unbeknownst to everyone but me, Edmund had joined the tour once we got to my room. He was pleased by Grandma Deena's excessive enthusiasm, and I was glad that it gave at least one person pleasure. Of course, Edmund was outraged by Grandpa Don's disapproval, but he calmed down when the consensus was overwhelmingly positive.

I ended the tour in the kitchen, just as everyone was getting hungry. Grandma Sondra ran around with my dad, getting the food ready. Grandpa Sam helped me set the table, while my mom tended to drinks. Grandma Deena sat her self at the table and declared we were having a feast fit for a prince. By which, she meant me. I know, because when she said "prince" she pinched my cheek which was in range as I put down the napkins.

When Putnam Market's grilled chicken, salad, sliced tomatoes, mozzarella, and fresh bread were on the table, the rest of us sat down. Edmund stood close by, breathing in.

Grandpa Don asked me, "How are you doing in school?"

Grandma Deena said, "How do you think he's doing? He's a brilliant boy."

Grandpa Don cut her off, "I was asking Timmy. So?"

I answered, "I'm doing pretty well. It's not as challenging here as Scarsdale, but that leaves me more time to read."

My mom said proudly, "As I told you on the phone, Timmy skipped two grades in English and History and one grade in Spanish."

Grandpa Don said, "And what about Math and Science? Those are the most important subjects. In my day, I was the best math student in the high school, not just the grade. Understanding math will make you a good businessman."

Grandma Sondra had to jump in, "Maybe Tim doesn't want to be a businessman. There are lots of other things to be. It's important for him to discover his interests and talents and then use them. And when he does, he'll go far."

Grandma Deena said, "Whatever Tim does, he'll be the best in the world, bar none. And when you're rich as Croesus, Timmy, you'll take good care of your grandma who believed in you."

Grandpa Sam said, "Tim, just remember that riches are all well and good, but true happiness is even better." He gave Grandma Sondra, who was sitting on his right, a kiss on the cheek.

Grandpa Don said, "We all know you have some problems socializing, Tim. Have you made any friends?"

Grandma Sondra looked horrified, "What kind of question is that, Don?"

I said, "It's fine, Grandma. I actually have made one good friend." I smiled over at Edmund who grinned back at me.

"You have?" asked my dad.

"Oh, you don't know him, but he's a really good kid."

"Well, be sure to bring him around sometime. We'd love to meet him," said my mom.

Grandma Deena said, "Any friend of Tim's is a friend of mine. I like him already."

To stop the inevitable flood of questions, I asked my grandparents how their studies were going. Through their housing center, they were all enrolled in college courses. Of course, Grandma Deena was wild about school, Grandpa Don hated it, and the Cohens found it interesting and challenging. At least it was a subject that all four could discuss without focusing on me.

After lunch, we cleared the kitchen table and played Scrabble in teams, with me joining my parents. My team won because we had an unfair advantage. Edmund proved himself the worthy son of a wordsmith, although he had never played before. I wanted him to stop giving me seven letter words, but I couldn't speak to him. I couldn't even ignore his advice because, when I tried to, he got tearful. We played until tea time, then Dad got out the muffins, and we moved into the living room.

Dad cleared his throat before saying, "Tim, as I mentioned earlier today, your grandparents have an important matter to discuss with you." He motioned to Grandma Sondra.

She said, "Tim dear, you know that we all love you very much."

Grandma Deena interrupted, "That's too mild. You are the light of our life. Without you, all would be darkness."

Grandpa Sam said, "And because you mean so much to us, we have tried to secure a comfortable future for you, as best we could."

Grandma Sondra said, "So when you were born, we established a trust fund for you."

Grandpa Donald muttered, "It still bothers me that we did it so soon. What if he had grown up to be one of those hooligans or a cult member? All that money would have been tied up in his name. He still could turn out bad. I don't want my money going to the Hare Krishnas."

Grandma Deena said, "If Tim is a Hare Krishna, then I'll be a Hare Krishna, and they can have all my money, too."

Grandpa Sam, trying to get the conversation back on track, said, "Tim, the trust fund exists, but the money won't be yours to spend until you're thirty. In the meantime, your parents, as trustees, have the power to make investments."

My mom spoke up. "This is where we come in. Your father and I believe we've found an investment with enormous upside and little risk. But we don't want to do anything without your approval." She took a deep breath and said, "We want you to buy Chatsworth Mansion."

I gasped and so did Edmund. Never in my wildest dreams had I thought such a thing was possible. I didn't even think my parents could afford to buy a house.

My mother continued, "The house is an incredible bargain for a crazy reason. Remember how the house was used as an inn for haunted house fans?" I nodded. "Well, have you heard the rumor that the house really was and still is haunted?"

I said, "I've heard that mentioned once or twice."

Edmund rolled his eyes.

My dad said, "Fortunately, we're rational and know that ghosts don't exist. We figure that if normal people live in the house for a period of time, the rumors will die."

I said, "So, to make your plan work, we would have to live here for several years?"

My dad answered, "The bare minimum would be four, which would be perfect, because that would take you through high school."

I said, "Do you and mom want to stay put for four years? That would be unprecedented."

My mother answered, "There are lots of reasons for us to stay. Dad and I love our jobs, you're doing well in school, and the house is solid and spacious. Also, Dad and I aren't so young anymore, and we feel ready to put down some roots."

"Let's say I'm willing to stay here for four years, then what?" I asked.

My dad took this round. "Then you can sell the house and make a tidy profit, or you can go off to college and charge your mother and me rent."

Grandpa Don stuck his oar in. "What makes you think the house will sell at a profit? As far as I can tell, it's a white elephant. Too big and too ugly for anyone in his right mind to buy."

Edmund's face went red.

My dad said, "Granted, Dad, it's big. But the top floor can be shut off. And it's ugly because of the god-awful color. We've seen an old photo of the house in its original light brown, and it's quite handsome. If we paint the outside and dispel the rumors, this house should be worth two, maybe even three, times what Tim pays for it. I predict it will be a good investment."

I asked all my grandparents what they thought. Grandma Sondra thought it was a splendid idea, but only if I would be happy living in Saratoga. Grandpa Sam, of course, agreed. Grandma Deena thought it was the best plan she had ever heard in her life. Grandpa Don thought it was the worst.

I looked at six hopeful faces—that's all my relatives, with the exception of Grandpa Don, plus Edmund—and was persuaded. If someone had told me the evening before that I would willingly consign myself to living in Saratoga for four years, I would have told him that he was nuts. But meeting Edmund had changed a lot. Even if I was miserable at school, I felt certain I would be happy at home.

My mother said, "Oh, there's something else to sweeten the pot. Your father and I were hesitant to pursue the purchase because we didn't want to deal with Ellen Stilton. But at the party last night, we met a wonderful realtor. She and her husband were dressed as fellow Victorians, Robert and Elizabeth Browning. This realtor, well, she's a part-time realtor and a part-time lawyer, said that only Dad and I were Ellen Stilton's clients. Since you would be the purchaser, Tim, you would be free to engage this nice woman."

If I felt like I had stepped into a Charles Chatsworth novel because I had suddenly gone from rags to riches, imagine how I felt when, in response to my inquiry about the new realtor's name, my mother said, "Julia Green. She has a daughter at the high school. Have you ever met her? I think her name is Emma.

Chapter Sixteen

I had to wait a long time to look for Chatsworth's diary. My grandparents stayed for dinner and, afterwards, my parents worked in the library until bedtime. I had hoped to sneak a peek in the morning, but Edmund and I stayed up late whispering, so I overslept and had to race to catch the bus. Then I had to endure the entire day at school. Actually, I should qualify that statement. Although I was eager to get home, school wasn't so bad. A few kids asked leading questions like, "How was your Halloween, Bite Size?" Instead of ignoring them or responding sullenly, I said it was great, which seemed to take the wind out of my inquisitors' sails. Between meeting Edmund and learning I was rich enough to buy a house, I was feeling pretty happy and it showed.

When, late in the afternoon, I walked through the mansion's back door, Edmund was waiting for me, bursting with impatience. He had spent the entire day in the library, dreaming of the diary, without being able to extract it. I threw together a sandwich of the leftover grilled chicken and bread, and then Edmund and I raced to the library.

"Tell me again which drawer it is," I said, chewing.

"The bottom right hand drawer. Just open it. You don't even have to remove it."

I opened the drawer which looked perfectly normal.

I said, "I don't see anything. Are you sure this is the one?"

"Maybe you should have put on your deerstalker cap to help you think. Look at the wood about three inches back on the right hand side."

As directed, I looked and I saw an indentation, a moon-shaped cut-out about the size of a fingernail.

Edmund said, "Put your index fingernail into that slot and pull up."

I did so, and the entire thin "bottom" of the drawer lifted up. Underneath lay a slender black leather diary and a larger black book labeled "Household Accounts." I removed both books and put the false bottom back in place.

I asked, "How did you know about this secret storage? Did you spy on your father?"

"Certainly not," said Edmund indignantly. "My father showed me his secret drawer because he was sickly. If anything had happened to him, I was to run the household."

"Didn't you want to read his diary to see how he felt about Hattie?"

"Tim, I'm surprised at you. On Saturday night, you said you were a man of honor, and I believe that you are. As such, you know that I would never have trespassed on my father's private thoughts. To be perfectly honest, I would prefer not to do so now, but I see that we must to clear his name."

For the unveiling, I suggested that we go up to our bedroom. Although both my parents were out, my mother occasionally came home early to work in the library where the Victorian ambiance was "inspiring." I didn't want her to find me reading aloud to myself.

Up in our room, we assumed our usual places, with me on my bed and Edmund on the butterfly chair. I was nervous about reading the diary to Edmund without skimming it first. What if it revealed his father to be a monster who had plotted his son's murder? If it did, Edmund would be crushed. Concealing my true concern, I asked if I could read the diary to myself to get familiar with the difficult handwriting. Understandably, Edmund would have none of it; he didn't want to wait a second longer.

I opened the well-preserved book carefully and turned to the final entry dated November 24, 1879. Edmund told me this was a few weeks after his own death and just a couple of weeks before his father's.

I read aloud:

My life force seems to be slipping away, and no amount of tonic restores me. But what care I? Wouldst that I could be as brave as my darling Edmund and end my own wretched existence. To approach the edge of darkness and fall into the abyss...'tis a consummation devotedly to be wished. Yet I am a terrible coward and cannot do the deed. Still, it matters little. I shall shuffle off this mortal coil ere long and then reside eternally in Heaven with my dearest Margaret, my darling Harold, and my beloved Edmund.

But when that blessed day comes, how shall I face dear Edmund whom I have injured so gravely? I shall fall to my knees and beg his forgiveness for bringing such unhappiness into our lives. Had I consulted with the Brothers Grimm, I could not have conjured a more evil stepmother. It pains me to my very core to think of her words on the day of Edmund's burial. I had complained of the rector's refusal to provide a proper service and of his insistence on a burial in the dark of night with no friends present. In response, Hattie said, "You are lucky that Edmund was buried in sacred ground at all. When I was growing up in the countryside, suicides were not allowed such consideration, and with good reason." Oh the cruelty of her words. As if a father burying his beloved child could ever be deemed "lucky." And the malice of begrudging Edmund even an imperfect burial which, I am afraid, will not afford him an easy rest.

I fear I am losing my mind, but I feel compelled to leave a message to my son in case his spirit should ever stumble upon these words:

My dearest Edmund, You were a constant source of joy to me. I loved you more than words can say, and I gladly would have given my own life in place of yours. If you have been denied peace, I hope you shall find it soon, and then please hurry to join Momma and Harold and me. We would be so glad to be with you once again.

I closed the diary, but didn't dare to look up. I could hear Edmund quietly crying. I grabbed a tissue from my nightstand and blew my nose.

When Edmund's sniffles subsided, I said quietly, "I'm sorry I ever doubted your father, Edmund. He was the best of fathers and the best of men."

"You needn't apologize, Tim. If you hadn't doubted my father, we would never have retrieved his diary. Receiving my father's message is the best thing that has happened to me since my death. Even if we don't ever discover who murdered me, my existence will be easier henceforth."

"Don't give up on our investigation yet. We still have two prime suspects and now we have invaluable help from primary sources." I held up the two volumes.

Edmund asked, "What can we learn from the household accounts besides how much was spent on mutton and on cravats?"

"We won't know until we look. Shall we?"

I moved over to the desk, turned on the lamp, pushed aside some books and papers, and spread the book open. Edmund insisted that I sit in the chair while he stood over my shoulder. The ledger contained meticulously maintained, highly detailed records of household expenditures, all written in the same neat hand as the diary. There were several vertical columns, each labeled across the top as follows: date of payment, item or salary, vendor or employee, amount paid. Each row down contained an entry.

"This is amazing," I said. "It's a wonder your father had time to do anything else."

"As you can see, my father took accounting seriously. He started out life with little money and had to watch his spending carefully. Even when he had plenty of money, he didn't stop watching."

"I know," I said, "In your family, old habits die hard."

Edmund smiled. "Accounting especially appealed to his personality. He was highly organized and sensitive to detail. Had he not been, he couldn't have written his novels, especially not in serialization."

"I'm not sure that I follow you." I turned the page and kept scanning the records while we talked.

"In my father's day, many of the popular novelists, like Charles Dickens, George Eliot, William Thackeray and my father, wrote novels in installments which were published, either weekly or monthly, in regular magazines or as "part issues" whose sole content was a section of the novel. Once an installment came out, the writer could not go back and make changes. The writer had to know from the outset what characters and plot twists he would introduce along the way. Being organized and aware of details was not just helpful to my father's work, it was essential. My father always stayed an installment or two ahead of his deadlines, but Charles Dickens was infamous for falling behind. On one occasion, Dickens was so tardy that as he finished writing each page, he handed it directly to the printer for type setting."

"I never really thought of how difficult writing in installments was."

"It was difficult and not just because of deadlines. To keep people buying, the plots had to be constantly exciting. Readers would get so intrigued that they would line up to buy the newest installment and then would talk of nothing else until the next installment arrived."

"Kind of like today's suspenseful television shows."

"What are 'television shows'?" asked Edmund.

"I'm almost in the dark as much as you, coming from the only family in America without a television, or two, or ten.

But, to the best of my knowledge, a television is a little box that allows you to see theatrical performances." Edmund was still looking blank. "Remind me to show you some clips on the computer, so you can see for yourself. Trust me, though, people today are as crazy about serialized TV shows as they were in your day about serialized novels."

We had scanned several pages, covering a few months in 1878. I paged ahead to see the last entries which were in early December 1879. Edmund said, "I had no idea that clothing cost so much and servants cost so little, but I don't see anything relevant to our inquiry, do you?"

"Perhaps. Did you notice that every week, there's an entry for 'HFC'?"

"My stepmother."

"Yes, Hattie Fields Chatsworth. Her allowance was quite substantial."

Edmund said, "It was not unusual for the wife of a wealthy man to receive an allowance."

"That may be, but I wonder what she was spending it on. If you look closely at the entries, every need of hers was met, including servants, food, drink, shelter, furniture, linens, knick-knacks, dresses, hats, jewelry, and even spa visits. Did she have any relatives to support?"

"Not to my knowledge. Both her father and mother died when she was young. At the wedding, the only relative from her side was her son."

"How did she spend her days?"

"She was a lady of leisure. She paid social calls and received them. She gave glittering dinner parties. She went to the spa for the waters. She attended theater and horse races. She read a little and embroidered less. Oh, and she fancied herself an excellent distiller of herbs."

"She had a stillroom, right?"

"She did. Although most of my father's friends had converted their stillrooms to pantries, Hattie wanted one. My father had the stillroom built in the basement where it was dry, warm, and dark. Hattie claimed that, between her tonics and the Saratoga waters, my father would be cured."

"So the tonic your father mentioned in his diary was made by Hattie?"

"Yes. And not only my father took her tonic. She insisted that I do so, too."

"Do you have any idea what she put in her tonic?"

"Herbs from the garden, but I don't know which ones. She grew a great variety of them."

"I know," I said. "On the day that I dug up your spectacles, I found markers for her garden."

"That won't tell us too much about the tonic's ingredients. She used her herbs for many things other than tonics, like perfumes and cordials."

"Did you ever see her recipe book?"

"No, I didn't. I never set foot in the stillroom. I did everything in my power to stay as far away from Hattie as possible. That was part of the attraction of the widow's walk: Hattie was in the basement and I was on the roof."

"I know where the key to the stillroom is. Shall we head to the basement and take a look around?" I asked.

"I'm all in favor of the expedition, but aren't we supposed to be investigating Albert next?"

"Fortunately, this investigation isn't a serialized novel and, so, we can make changes to our plan. I'm afraid that the push from the roof may have been the second attempt on your life; the first may have been concocted in the stillroom."

113

Chapter Seventeen

I should have known that, as soon as I made a plan for the next step of the investigation, it would be thwarted. Sherlock Holmes never had to deal with disruptions from school and parents. Edmund and I had only gotten half-way down the main staircase when my dad came through the front door. He was carrying a small box of books, their green gilded covers peeking out from the top. Before the bookstore had closed, he had stopped by to pay the balance and to pick up the additional thirteen volumes.

I went out to the car to bring in the other box of books, while Edmund followed my father. Having carried the heavy box into the library, I found my dad dusting off books and putting them onto an empty shelf. As I had predicted, they looked mighty fine. Edmund was smiling broadly.

"This is quite a set of books you bought, Tim," said my dad. "They'll inspire me to get cracking on my novel. If Chatsworth could write this much in long-hand, I should be able to get something down with the miracle of word processing."

"Long-hand was the least of his problems, Dad. Chatsworth's novels were serially published, so he had to plan everything in advance. Once an installment came out, there was no going back to fix details."

"How do you know these things? Now I don't know whether to be inspired or depressed. Oh, before I forget, this is for you." My dad reached into the big pocket of his tweed jacket and pulled out a thin, green leather bookmark with gilt decoration. "Your friend at the bookstore sent it. She said that when you read Chatsworth, you should mark your place with this to preserve the binding. She also said you should stop by any time, even if you're not looking for anything special."

Like I said, she was cracked, but in a good way. "Thanks for the bookmark, and thanks for picking up the books. The house feels more complete now."

"Yes, it does. And the house will feel even better once we paint it, which we'll do once we own it. Which reminds me, we owe Julia Green a call. We've got to get the ball rolling." He reached into his pocket again. This time he pulled out a business card and handed it to me. "Why don't you call first, and then I'll take over," he said. He went back to unpacking, dusting, and shelving.

"Do you really think I should call, Dad? I mean, she'll want to talk to you as the trustee. I don't know anything about buying homes. I could barely buy a set of books."

"You're the customer, Tiny Tim. It's important for you to be involved."

"Ok, if you say so." I know it sounds ridiculous, but as soon as I saw the name "Julia Green" on the card, I felt a little breathless, as if I were calling Emma herself. The card listed both Mrs. Green's office and home number. I tried the office number first; it rang through to the answering machine.

"She's not at the office," I told my dad.

"Then try her at home. She said you should feel free to call her there."

As I punched in the number, I didn't know whether to wish for Emma to pick up or not. The phone rang, was picked up, and a voice said, "Hello." It was neither Emma nor her mother. It was a little girl's voice. Emma's little sister.

"Hello. This is Tim Ross. Is your mother available?"

"Yes," she said. There was a long pause in which I could hear her breathing.

I finally said, "May I speak with her."

She said, as if my request was unexpected, "Oh, sure."
Then she called loudly into the receiver, "Mom. Telephone."

In a few seconds, Mrs. Green picked up. "Hello. This is
Julia Green." The little sister dropped the receiver back into
the cradle with a crash.

My hands started to sweat. "Hi. This is Tim Ross. I'm
the...boy, I mean...man, I mean...person interested in buying
Chatsworth Mansion. My dad said it was ok to call you at
home, but if this is a bad time, we can talk later, Mrs.
Green."

"This is a good time and, please, call me Julia. That is, if
you feel comfortable. Or you can call Ermitrude, if you like."

"Is that your real name?"

"No, but you can call me it."

I liked her already. What she said next made me like her
a lot more.

"Tim, I understand that you go to Saratoga High. I took
the liberty of asking my daughter Emma if she knew you,
and she said that I had to tell you, 'Here's looking at you,
kid.' Are you a Bogart fan?"

"Pretty much," I said. Humphrey Bogart was the lead
actor in the movie *Casablanca* that Emma and I had quoted
from at the Stiltons. Bogart says the line "Here's looking at
you, kid," to Ingrid Bergman, his long-lost love, when she
wanders back into his life. The saying, which is kind of
enigmatic, has come to mean, "I make a toast to you because
you're special to me." I was so happy. Emma liked me.
Maybe not I'll-be-your-girlfriend kind of like, but definitely
I'll-be-your-friend kind of like.

Before I could respond Julia was saying, "The first step to
buying a house usually involves my showing you the house
but, unless you feel insufficiently acquainted with the
closets, we can move on to the next step, which is a formal
offer to the sellers. As you probably know, they're very
motivated, having had the house on the market for several

years. I would recommend that you start very low. Who knows, they may be so desperate that they'll pay *you* to take it off their hands. Your father and I will work on strategy."

"Great, he's actually standing right here. Would you like to talk to him?"

"Sure, in a second. First, do you have any questions?"

"Just one." Something had popped into my mind.

"Shoot."

"When you speak to Emma, could you tell her that I said, 'We'll always have Paris.'?"

"More *Casablanca*, huh? I'd be happy to tell her, but why don't you tell her yourself? At the rate we're going, I'll end up repeating the entire screenplay."

My mind was racing. Tell her myself? Where? When? How? Would telling her get me beaten up? Did I care?

Once again, Julia saved me from having to respond. She said, "If you're interested, Emma would like to meet you at Wheat Fields, tomorrow night at seven o'clock."

"You mean, we'd meet Tuesday night for dinner?"

"That's her suggestion since she's off from ballet then, but if you prefer a different place, a different time, a different planet, she's game."

"No, Wheat Fields tomorrow at seven would be great."

"Good. I'll tell Emma. Oh, and she said to be sure to wear a deerstalker and a cape so she'll recognize you."

I was kind of in shock, so I blithered, "Right. Well, thanks. Thanks a lot. Very nice to meet you. Well, not really meet you, but speak to you. And tell Emma I'm really looking forward to dinner. Well, not the dinner itself, to seeing her. Ok, here's my dad now."

My dad took the phone from me and started discussing opening offers. I headed upstairs with Edmund.

Once the door was closed, I said, "For two months I've dreamed of this day."

"This girl Emma is very nice, I suppose?"

"She's better than nice. She's beautiful and funny and smart and kind and warm."

"Then what does she want with you?" he asked, jokingly.

I couldn't joke. "I really don't know. She's been going out with this super-popular, ultra-handsome guy named Jared. He's even a sophomore. Maybe she wants to make him jealous. Or maybe she's just helping her mother's business...some kids do that. Maybe it isn't really a date. I mean, who goes out on a Tuesday night? Dinner on Tuesday is probably the same as coffee on Saturday, but I don't know the ranking system."

"Perhaps it hasn't been proposed as a serious date, but perhaps it will become one. If you truly like this girl, which appears to be the case, then you should try to woo her."

"How can I do that? I'm not exactly the wooing type. I'm probably two inches shorter than she is and not very experienced. Actually, not at all experienced."

"This advice may sound hackneyed, but just be yourself. Oh, and avoid onions and garlic at dinner."

"How do you know? Did you ever have a girlfriend?" I asked.

Tears sprang to his eyes again. He spoke haltingly. "There was a lovely girl named Lucy back in England. She was my third cousin on my mother's side. I loved her dearly, and she returned my feelings. We had come to an understanding regarding a future together, but we never told anyone. How I hated leaving England to come here, knowing that an ocean would divide me from my beloved. I never saw her again."

"Do you know what became of her?"

"I don't. I like to think that my death touched her, but did not ruin her. I fear that my 'suicide' made her question the strength of my love and commitment. But I hope that she found love again and had children and grandchildren and a happy life."

Edmund's generosity struck me keenly.   Instead of wanting Lucy to spend the rest of her life pining for him, he wished her a full life. Maybe love made you act like that, made you want what was best for the other person, even if it wasn't what was best for you. I vowed that I would act that way with Emma. I would be her friend and want what was best for her, even if that didn't include me. I would make my bid, but if she wasn't interested, I'd back off.

"Edmund, do you really think I have a shot at getting Emma?"

"Edgar got his Angelina, didn't he? I think will get your Emma."

Chapter Eighteen

It's funny how, when you have the right key for the lock, opening a door is no big deal. Edmund was standing right behind me as I effortlessly opened the stillroom. It's also funny how a new way of life can become a routine in just a couple of days. As part of my typical new existence, I had gone to school in the morning, gotten through the day with little hassle, finished my homework on the bus, and returned home to find Edmund waiting for me. He was eager to go to the stillroom. To be honest, I wanted to put off the stillroom in favor of the attic. After months of waiting, I had finally gotten into the attic on Saturday, and now it was Tuesday and I still hadn't been back there to trawl for treasure. Unfortunately, there wasn't enough time for me to investigate both the basement and the attic before I had to get ready for my big date...or little date...or no date ...whatever dinner was.

But as soon as I saw Edmund's expectant face, I knew that the attic would have to wait. And so, after I ate a snack, we headed down the basement stairs and through the little rooms to the stillroom.

As the stillroom door opened, it creaked even louder than the attic door, as if protesting our invasion. The room looked like it hadn't been touched since Hattie had last occupied it. It still smelled faintly of dried herbs, and it was, as required, dark and warm. No electrical lighting had been installed. Before we had descended, Edmund had told me to grab a box of safety matches, which I had done without questioning. Now I found out why. The stillroom had two overhead light fixtures which worked on pulleys. Edmund instructed me to lower each fixture, to lift up its glass chimney, to turn the side knobs to raise the two side-by-side wicks, to light the wicks which were fueled by paraffin, and to replace the glass chimney. This lighting system seemed archaic to me, but Edmund explained that when the house was built, the "duplex burner" was the latest thing.

Once the fixtures were lit, we could see the room quite clearly. There was a large wooden table in the center, with a long wooden bench on one side. Along the far wall, there were built-in shelves, from floor to ceiling, for storage. The shelves still held the key stillroom equipment: baskets for gathering herbs, mortar and pestles for grinding, wooden bowls for mixing, dozens of labeled wooden boxes and glass jars filled with herbs, and glass bottles filled with tinctures and oils. Off to the left was a large sink and, near it, a wood burning stove with a large copper still on top. Off to the right, hanging near the ceiling, was a drying rack to hang herbs, which could be raised or lowered by pulleys.

I said, "This was quite an elaborate operation!"

"Yes, Hattie was proud of her stillroom."

"I don't see the recipe book, do you?"

"No, but you wouldn't expect it to be in plain sight."

"Right," I said, "Let's start with the drawer."

There was a drawer in the center of the big table which I opened, but all I found was string, scissors, knives, wooden and metal spoons, and some labels. I pulled out the drawer and carefully checked every inch of it for a false bottom. No luck. I walked over to the shelves and looked under all the baskets. Nada.

I said, "Hattie probably took the book with her when she left."

"Perhaps she did, but I watched Hattie and Albert leave that moonlit night, and they had very little with them. Let's check more thoroughly."

I concentrated on looking up and down each long shelf. I particularly focused on the labels to see if there was arsenic or some other poison. My careful scrutiny yielded neither the book nor any obvious lethal agents, but because I was small, I hadn't seen the top shelf.

"I want to get a look up there." I pointed upwards. I dragged over the heavy wooden bench, wishing that Edmund could help me. I climbed up and looked at the shelf.

"Bingo!" I cried, and Edmund smiled.

I took down a brown cloth-covered book, dusty, but intact. After I pushed the bench back into place, Edmund and I sat down, side by side, and I opened the book. Across the top, each page was clearly marked with a recipe heading. There were recipes for perfumes, colognes, cordials, tonics, and liniments. Many of the tonics were for specific ailments, like "blood impurities," "female ills," and "heartburn, dyspepsia, and cramps," but one tonic said "for general health and well-being." Since that page looked well-worn, we concluded that this was Hattie's special tonic. We carefully read through the ingredients, but found nothing harmful.

"I still think that some strange ingredient affected you, Edmund. Can you tell me when your symptoms started and what they were?"

Edmund said, "They started soon after we arrived here in Saratoga. In England, I felt fine. My change of health was just another reason to resent our transplantation. My symptoms were similar to my father's: dizziness, nausea, restlessness, insomnia, tremors. I escaped to the roof often because, up there, I could breathe easier. But as time went on, I became sicker and sicker, and, sometimes, I could see and hear my dead brother and mother. It was terrifying. I thought I was losing my mind as well as my body."

"And when did you start taking the tonic? Was it when you came to the United States?"

"Yes it was. My father had begun taking it in England, once he married Hattie. She had urged me to take it, too, saying that I would be susceptible to the same ailments as my father. I had refused, but when we got here I felt so low and listless that I gave in to her. You must remember, almost everyone took tonics and pills in those days. My father said Charles Dickens swore by Dr. Fowler's Cure-all Tonic. My father was pleased that he didn't have to buy a commercial product, but instead had a homemade one."

"How did the tonic taste?"

"Absolutely awful. Imagine the worst thing you ever put in your mouth and then make it ten times worse. Every time I took a spoonful, it made me shudder."

"Isn't it odd that you experienced symptoms once you took the tonic and that, over time, the symptoms got much worse? Your initial low spirits could well have been depression, nothing more. I'm convinced that the tonic was making you and your father sick, although I must admit, I don't see any harm in the recipe besides the foul taste."

"Maybe Hattie added something to the mixture that she didn't write down," offered Edmund.

"Of course. That's what she did. Edmund, you're brilliant! Now we just have to figure out what it was."

Edmund smiled broadly. "Maybe we should start by looking at the labels on the boxes and jars."

"Brilliant again!" The herbs were lined up alphabetically, with many more containers than there had been garden plants. Hattie must have bought some of her herbs from outside sources. We started at anise and worked our way down the row through dill and horehound and lavender. By the time we reached peppermint I was feeling pretty discouraged. Everything seemed so familiar and benign. We passed over sage and sorrel and finally landed at wormwood and yarrow. I remembered wormwood from the markers; it had been the only plant that I had never heard of.

"What was wormwood used for?" I asked.

"I believe it was a key ingredient in the cordial absinthe."

The name sounded vaguely familiar to me, but I couldn't think why. "Did Hattie make absinthe?"

"She did, lots of it, although my father didn't drink a drop. The drink was very popular among some of his writer and artist friends."

Artist friends. Suddenly I knew where I had heard of absinthe. In my eighth grade paper on van Gogh, I had written about his addiction to the green liquor. Some scholars believed that absinthe had caused him to see the strange swirls he depicted in his paintings and that, during a drunken binge, had driven him to cut off his ear.

"We've got to go read about wormwood on the Internet," I said to Edmund.

"Let's do a Google search," he responded. Edmund's old habits might die hard, but you sure could teach him new tricks.

I lowered the lamps and extinguished the flames. Then I grabbed the book and locked the stillroom behind us. We headed up the two flights of stairs to our room.

Sure enough, our Google search showed that dried wormwood was a powerful drug. It could cause all sorts of symptoms including indigestion, hallucinations, vertigo, insomnia, nausea, tremors, psychosis, and increased risk of suicide. In the United States, absinthe had been banned since the early 1900s.

"The tonic must have contained wormwood. That would account for all of your terrible symptoms," I said.

Edmund began to shake. "Then Hattie must have been my murderer, and my father's, too."

I wanted to agree with him and to feel the triumph of discovery, but something didn't feel right. I said to Edmund, "It sure looks like Hattie's guilty, although I still have some lingering questions."

He said, "What questions could you possibly have?"

"To begin with, why was Hattie giving the drug to your father and you?"

"Isn't that apparent? If she disposed of us both, she would inherit a vast estate."

"But why was she trying to kill your father first, and not you? Wasn't your father an excellent meal ticket for her? Wouldn't it have made sense for her to get rid of you first?"

"Don't forget," said Edmund, "That I refused to take the tonic in England, whereas my father was willing."

"But once you did start, why did she chance detection by pushing you off the roof?"

"These are important questions, but I have one for you."

"What's that?"

"Are you going to have enough time to shower and change before your date?"

I looked at the clock. It was now 6:15. I heard the front door open and close.

"Hey, Tiny Tim, I'm home," called my father. "What time do we set sail?"

I called down to him, "Give me twenty minutes, Dad. I need to get ready."

It took me somewhat longer because I had trouble combing my hair—where was my part supposed to go?—and couldn't decide on an outfit. Khakis with a shirt and sweater were the obvious choice, but which shirt and which sweater? Nothing seemed to match, or if they matched, they didn't fit. I finally settled on a white button down shirt and a navy sweater. Boring, but safe.

As I was putting on my socks, my mom knocked and came in.

"Hi, Tim, you look nice."

"Thanks, Mom.

"Are you excited?"

"I guess so."

"Nervous?"

"Should I be?" I suddenly had butterflies in my stomach. In fact, they felt so big, they were probably bats. But I wouldn't mention that to my mother.

"Of course you shouldn't. You are going to have a great time. I just wanted to give you a little advice, from the feminine viewpoint. Be yourself. If this Emma is a good, smart girl, she won't be able to resist you. Oh, and stay away from garlic and onions."

Clearly, advice to the lovelorn hadn't changed much in over a hundred years. I guess it's like they say in *Casablanca*, "The fundamental things apply as time goes by."

Chapter Nineteen

There was a guy sitting alone at the back corner table at the restaurant. That guy was me. I had wanted to arrive second, to make a grand entrance with Emma waiting at the table, but my dad would have none of my dallying. I think he was more nervous than I. Dad had insisted on driving me, ostensibly because it was too cold to bike, but really because he wanted to dispense words of wisdom while I was held hostage in the front seat.

"Listen, Timmy, I don't know much about this dating business. Your mother and I met when we were very young, and I never had eyes for anybody else. However, I do know something about friendship. I know that the best friends are the ones who know the real you and like that person. So, when you're with Emma tonight, make sure that you're funny and sweet and smart."

In other words, be yourself. I was getting the message. We parked in front of the restaurant. Dad said, "This is for you." He reached into his wallet and took out two twenties. "It will be a nice gesture for you to pay on the first date. I know kids these days like to split the bill. But every now and then, it's important to be generous and gracious."

"Well thanks, Dad, for being generous and gracious so I can be generous and gracious." I took the money. "I'll call you when I need to be picked up."

"Fine, we'll be waiting by the phone." Which, frighteningly, would be true.

As I was getting out of the car, he said, "Don't forget to steer clear of...."

"Onions and garlic," I said.

"How do you know these things, Timmy?"

The restaurant was Tuesday-night empty. I wanted to wait for Emma by the front, but the hostess insisted on seating me, as if in the next ten minutes all the tables would fill-up. Before the hostess left she said, "Your server tonight will be Shari."

I took a look around. The restaurant was pleasant, casual and attractive. The perfect place for a non-date date. I checked my watch. I was five minutes early, and Emma would probably be ten minutes late. Not out of malice, of course. Just because most normal people arrive ten minutes late. Fifteen minutes to kill. The bus boy poured some water into the two water glasses. I took a sip.

At a nearby table sat a little Japanese girl, maybe about three or four, with chin length black hair. She had finished eating, but her parents hadn't. She looked my way, and I smiled at her. Her face lit up with relief. Someone to play with. She climbed down off her chair.

"Where are you're going, Mariya?" her mother asked.

"I go to see the big boy," she answered.

Her mother looked over. "Do you mind?"

"Nah. I'm just waiting for a friend."

Now it was the mother's face that lit up with relief. Mariya raced over.

I said, "Hi, Mariya, my name is Tim."

"You know my name. Are you my friend?" she asked.

"I'd like to be."

"Ok, you can be." I wished everyone were so easy. After about ten minutes of trying to entertain Mariya, I was re-thinking my position. Finally, we found a game to play: I recited "round and round the garden I lost my teddy bear" as I traced circles on her palm, "I took one step, two steps" as my fingers stepped up her arm, "and found him under there!" as I tickled her under her arm. She insisted that I do it over and over. It never grew old for her. It stayed pretty fresh for me, too, because every time I tickled her, she let loose a real belly laugh.

"Can I have a turn?" I looked up. There was Emma, smiling like mad. She looked more beautiful than I remembered.

Mariya, intimidated by the competition, ran back to her table. Her mother waved at me and mouthed the words "thank you."

"Hi," was all I managed to say to Emma because I was smiling like mad, too.

"I'm ten minutes late, and you're already two-timing me."

I had to start talking. "Hey, can I help it if pretty girls throw themselves at me?"

"I suppose not. It's a tough job, but somebody's got to do it."

"Yup, I handle pretty girls and teddy bears. If you lose a teddy bear, I'm your man."

"I try to keep close tabs on my teddy bears but, just in case, it's good to know." She sat down. "Listen, I'm sorry I'm late. I hope I haven't kept you waiting too long."

I wanted to say, "all my life," but instead I said, "I have been waiting, but not because you're late. You're socially punctual. I'm just pathologically punctual, which means I always arrive at least ten minutes early."

"I like to be early, too, but the rehearsal for my recital went half an hour late. It's funny, but no matter how hard I try, I can't be in two places at once."

"Like my Grandma Sondra says, 'You can't dance at two weddings with one butt.'" Actually, she uses the Yiddish word "tuchas" but I wasn't sure that would fly in Saratoga.

"My grandma Ethel says the same thing, only she says 'tuchas.'" Emma continued, "Our grandmothers are wise women. But what if the butt is big enough? Maybe a big butt could dance at two weddings."

"That is a nasty visual."

Saved by the waitress. "Hi, my name is..."

I interrupted, "Let me guess." I pretended to search for a vibe. "Is it Shari?"

"Yeah. That's awesome. Can you do that all the time?"

"Just when the other world speaks to me."

"Cool," she said, her eyes wide with wonder.

I had a feeling Shari would be telling all her friends about her psychic customer.

She got back to business. "As you know, I'm Shari and I'm going to be the server tonight...for you. Here's some bread ...for you." She put down a small basket with bread and whipped butter. "And special butter ...for you."

I thought I'd play it safe and ask, "What's special about the butter."

She responded, "It's garlic butter."

I was being tested, but I would not fail. "Could we have some plain?" I asked.

"Sure, I can get some plain butter...for you. Can I get any drinks...for you? Sparkling water?"

I looked at Emma. "How about some Saratoga Springs Water to toast our first outing?" Note, I did not refer to the dinner as a date. Pretty suave of me.

Emma said, "Sure. Bring out a bit of the bubbly...for us."

Shari said, "Here are the menus...for you." She handed us each one. "And I'll get the Saratoga Water...for you."

As soon as she was gone, Emma said, "If I snap and strangle her, it will be a case of justifiable homicide, right?"

"Either that, or the electric chair...for you." I opened my menu. "What do you recommend?"

"I would go with a pasta or a pasta or a pasta," she said. The Wheat Fields' menu had a note that all the breads and pastas were freshly made on the premises.

Shari came back with the butter, two glasses, and our Saratoga Water. She opened the blue bottle and poured some into our new glasses. Then she took out her pad and pen. "What can I get...for you?"

We ordered, both of us sticking to pastas, and then dug into the warm, soft bread.

"This bread is delicious," I said.

"Not up to the standards of cheese puffs, perhaps, but pretty great," she responded.

"Ah, cheese puffs," I extolled, "The food of the gods."

"I totally agree, although I prefer this setting to our cheese puff setting."

"Is that based on the quality of the décor or of the company?"

"Definitely the quality of the company. Which brings me to my point," she said. "You're probably wondering why I called you here today."

"I thought it was to get a carbo-high."

"That, and to discuss our past and our future." Suddenly, she sounded serious. "Tim, this is super-embarrassing, so please promise that you'll forget what I'm saying if you're not interested." She paused and took a deep breath. "I really like you. I know we hardly know each other, but I want to remedy that. I've been patient, waiting for you to call or to track me down, but two months have passed and I don't want to be patient anymore. I know I threw myself at you at the party and you didn't respond, but I thought I'd give it one more try."

Under the table, I was re-bruising my arms with pinches. But before I could say anything, Shari showed up again, this time with our house salads. I was about to take a bite when I realized there were raw onions on top. I removed them with my fork and noticed that Emma was removing hers also. I guess the no onion, no garlic rule was universal.

I wanted to shout to Emma that I was totally interested, but I thought that this time, if I wanted to live to be fifteen, I'd better find out about my competition. "What about Jared? I thought you two were an item."

She shook her head. "I never should have let things drag on with Jared. At the party, which was our two week anniversary, I overheard kids saying he was going to dump me. I was so forward with you because I thought I was a free agent. But seeing me with another guy made Jared reconsider his plans. He begged me to stay with him, and I decided to wait until you made your intentions clear. When you didn't do anything, I felt kind of crushed. So, I let Jared hang around. He's actually been very sweet and attentive, but boring."

The bus boy came to the table and, before I could stop him, poured some tap water into my Saratoga Water glass.

Emma said, "We didn't even get a chance to make a toast. Is it ruined?"

I took a sip. It was flat.

"You know, this water seems like the perfect metaphor for you and Jared."

"How's that?" she asked.

"Well, if you pour more bubbly water into a glass of bubbly water, it stays bubbly. But if you pour flat water into bubbly water, it all goes flat. I don't understand how you even started going out with Mr. Flat Water."

"I guess I was kind of flattered. Jared ran through all the 'pretty girls' in his grade and then moved on to freshmen. In his facebook, he ranks the girls in order of preference. It was my turn."

"How could you possibly want to be part of that idiocy?"

"At the time he asked me out, nobody else was asking. I thought it would be interesting, from a sociological standpoint, to go out with the school's most popular boy."

"Has it been interesting?"

"Not at all. I don't have a lot of free time, and I don't want to waste it. I kept trying to break up with Jared, but he kept pleading with me to stay. I'm not sure if he wanted what he couldn't have or if he really liked me. Whatever the reason, I've finally freed myself. I'd rather stay home and watch *Casablanca* alone than spend time with someone I don't really like."

"Maybe you could watch *Casablanca* and spend time with someone you like," I offered.

"That's exactly what I was hoping you'd say."

I couldn't resist quoting the last line of the movie since it was so fitting, "Louis, I think this is the beginning of a beautiful friendship."

Chapter Twenty

In less than a week's time, I had gone from being poor to being rich, from being friendless to being befriended, and from being lovesick to being beloved. Well, maybe the last statement is a bit of an exaggeration, but Emma and I definitely had a commitment to spend time together. And although I'm not the type to kiss and tell, I will say that, when I went to say goodnight to Emma, I was glad I had avoided the garlic and onions.

Even with all these exciting developments, I had to get up the next morning to go to school. That's the unfortunate reality of being a kid. But at least I knew the excitement would continue when I got home. Edmund and I had decided that we would finally explore the attic, hoping to find additional clues to explain Hattie's guilt.

The highlights of my school day came at the beginning and at the end. In the morning, Emma met my bus to say hello. Emma had been driven to school by her mother and had arrived in time to wait for me. As soon as we saw each other, we started doing that mad smiling thing. She came up and took my hand, and this time I was sure she squeezed it. Then she walked me to homeroom and, in front of everybody, gave me a hug goodbye. In the afternoon, on the bus ride home, I took out my homework, and a few of the kids around me followed suit. One kid from my math class asked me for help. His question marked the beginning of a new era in which it was acceptable to talk to me again.

Edmund, as ever, was waiting for me when I got home, and we went to our room to get the key to the attic. I was rifling through my sock drawer for the key when I came upon the slips of paper that I had found in the library desk on the first day. I had totally forgotten about them, and eagerly pulled them out to read.

"Edmund, were these characters in you father's books: Princess Elizabeth, Count Fleet and Emperor of Norfolk?"

"Not that I recall. I can't say that I remember every character in every book, but none of those names sounds familiar."

I studied the papers. "This isn't your father's handwriting, is it? I found these in his desk, so I had assumed they were his." I held the papers out for Edmund. Although the pen and ink was the same vintage as the diary and ledger, the handwriting hadn't the same neat sweep.

"This is definitely not my father's hand. It's not my hand, and it's not Hattie's. I remember her handwriting because, like everything else about her, it was very dramatic. It had large loops and many curlicues."

"Could it have been written by Albert?"

"It could have been, although I wasn't acquainted with his handwriting. What do you suppose these numbers mean?"

Written under each of the strange names was a number: 260, 340, and 225 respectively.

"I wish I knew. If we knew what the names meant, we might understand the numbers. What did Albert have to do with royal personages?"

"Nothing that I know of...unless," said Edmund, "they weren't people."

"What are you thinking?"

"I'm thinking that these could be the names of horses at the race track."

"Edmund, you're brilliant again. I'm sure they are. And the numbers must refer to amounts won or lost."

"If we're talking about Albert, I am certain they were losses. He was a big gambler, but not a successful one. On a number of occasions, I overheard him arguing with his mother about his spendthrift ways."

"You've just answered the question of what Hattie spent her allowance on. She's far from the first mother to carry the burden of a wastrel son. Did Albert do any work?"

"No, he never did, which irked my father who worked so hard. Although my father was willing to support Albert within the household, to feed and shelter and clothe him, he saw no reason to provide Albert with spending money. According to my father, at the age of nineteen, Albert should have been pursuing his education or working."

"Tell me again how Albert spent his days."

"He was very athletic. He rode horses and swam and row-ed on Saratoga Lake. He went to the horse races, and he chased pretty girls."

"Now I need to ask a totally unrelated question: did you and your father take tonic from the same bottle or separate ones?"

"Separate ones. Hattie said that our needs were slightly different, based on our different ages."

"And to the best of your knowledge, Hattie and Albert never took the tonic."

"When they had ailments, Hattie prescribed restoratives, but I'm quite certain that they never used the same daily tonic that my father and I did."

I was suddenly very excited. "I have to tell you a story from last night, Edmund."

Poor Edmund had already gotten quite an earful about my date with Emma. He was a good sport, though, and tried to look interested.

"Last night, Emma and I ordered Saratoga Springs bubbly water. The waitress poured the bottled water into glasses. Then the busboy came over and, before I could stop him, poured tap water into my bubbly water. I called over the waitress and explained that the water was now flat, but she couldn't see any difference. The busboy admitted his mistake, though, and the waitress brought us a new bottle."

"So, the story had a happy ending." Edmund was clearly trying to understand why I had bothered him with the dull account.

"It definitely did because it made me realize something essential to your case: Hattie was not the person putting wormwood in the tonic. Albert was. And, I believe, Albert pushed you off the roof. Albert was your murderer!"

Edmund collapsed into the butterfly chair. His voice was shaky. "Are you sure, Tim?"

"Unless Albert left a diary with a full confession, we'll never be a hundred percent sure. But the story makes sense if Albert is the culprit, not Hattie."

"What happened? I still don't understand."

"The restaurant story proves that, if a person serves a product, it can be tainted by a second person without the first person knowing. Hattie made the tonic, believing she was being helpful. She had no idea that Albert was secretly adding a dangerous ingredient. It was easy for him to do, with the stillroom so separate from the rest of the house. And because the tonic's taste was strong and unpleasant, the extra ingredient didn't stand out."

"When did Albert start tainting my father's tonic and why?"

"He started back in England. My guess is that, initially, he added just a little wormwood. His object was to make your father feel less vigorous so he would turn over the household accounts to Hattie. If Hattie controlled the books, and padded the accounts a bit, Albert would have an excellent source of pocket money. But Hattie didn't get control. Even when your father felt ill and demoralized, he was determined to keep the accounts."

"Why didn't Albert just kill my father by tampering?"

"At first, Albert probably refrained because he wasn't

swamped with debt and because his mother was so happy. Your father was unhappy in the marriage, but, as you yourself said, Hattie enjoyed the fame and fortune. As Mrs. Charles Chatsworth, she moved in the loftiest social circles. Without her husband by her side, she was nothing more than a failed actress."

"And later?"

"Later, when Albert amassed large debts and became desperate, he didn't kill your father because he understood that you had to be killed first. If your father died while you lived, you would inherit the bulk of the estate."

"Do you really think Albert became desperate enough to kill me?"

"He had enormous debts which his mother's allowance couldn't discharge. And Hattie had no other source of income."

"She had exquisite jewels," said Edmund.

"But she couldn't sell them. Your father would have noticed. Albert must have felt like your friend Tantalus: all the glories of riches around him, but only the superficial trappings within his reach. Except, if you and your father were gone."

"But if we were gone, it was Hattie, not Albert who would inherit the estate."

"True, but Hattie was an indulgent mother who denied Albert nothing. His mother having the money was as good as his having it in his own pocket."

"So, as soon as I agreed to take the tonic, Albert seized his opportunity?"

"Right. Since your tonic was separate, he gave you a larger dose of wormwood than your father. And he kept increasing the dose, causing your symptoms to worsen from restlessness to dizziness to hallucinations. But you hung on, and Albert grew impatient. He needed you to die first. He knew that you had taken to wandering the widow's walk and, remembering the novel's plot, followed it, but with a few minor improvements. He propped open the door, dispensed with a confession to the victim, and attacked from behind. He was an athletic man with powerful arms from swimming and rowing. It didn't take much for him to push you over."

"But why didn't he do it sooner? I was ill for quite some time."

"He was waiting for the perfect opportunity. He wanted a night when all the servants were out, so he wouldn't run into anyone on his way up to the attic or back down to his room. Don't forget, the servants all lived in the quarters on the third floor, but that night they were out at the fair. Undoubtedly, Albert would have been at the fair himself, being a *bon vivant*, but his evil plan kept him at home."

"Do you think he killed my father, too?"

"It's certainly possible that, after you were gone, he increased the dosage of wormwood. Your father wrote in his diary that he was very ill and worried about his sanity. But your father's deterioration could well have been the effects of a broken heart. He had lost so much with the deaths of your brother, your mother, and you, it's no wonder he lost the will to live."

"Did Hattie know of Albert's actions? Did she assist him?"

"No and no. For all her faults, Hattie wanted your father alive and well. Even when she had an opportunity to get rid of you--when you wanted to return to England--she fought to keep you here so your father would be happy."

"But she was so horrible about my suicide and would have denied me a proper burial."

"That was horrible, but it proves that she truly believed your death a suicide. If she had known that you were murdered, she wouldn't have dared to suggest that you be denied a sacred burial. That would have been blasphemous."

"I have one last question: why did Hattie, who inherited the entire fortune, steal away with Albert?"

"My guess is that something other than debts had gone wrong in Albert's life. Maybe he got a young lady pregnant and didn't want to marry her. Maybe he angered a dangerous man and feared for his life. Whatever it was, he was convinced that he had to flee, and wherever Albert went, Hattie was sure to follow. Of course, by leaving, Albert got the added benefit of escaping most of his debts. It was unlikely that any creditors would pursue their claims across the sea. And Hattie probably didn't mind leaving Saratoga by then. What she feared must have come to pass: her brilliant husband was dead and society was uninterested in the tiresome widow."

"So, it was all for money. My father and I were both sacrificed to satisfy Albert's debauched ways."

"I'm afraid so. If Albert is the murderer, everything makes sense, Edmund, in its terrible, nonsensical way."

Edmund was crying, again. I wanted to put my arms around him or at least hand him a tissue, but I couldn't.

I did the best I could by saying, "Edmund, I know this may sound crazy, but there's a part of me that's glad it happened."

Through his sobs, he said, "How can you say that?"

"Because if it hadn't happened, I never would have met you."

Chapter Twenty One

By the time Edmund calmed down, it was too late to go up to the attic. My mother was due home any moment, and the daylight had faded. I wasn't too disappointed, though; it had been an amazing day even without the treasure hunt. I had finally figured out what had happened at Chatsworth Mansion so long ago. Although the world wasn't holding its breath for the news, I had promised Edmund that I would try to get the word out.

I sat down at my computer and started writing an article about the murder. My fingers were flying as I put down all my thoughts. I wanted the article to follow the unraveled mystery from the presumption of suicide to the certainty of murder to the unmasking of the culprit. Edmund, reading over my shoulder, excitedly offered suggestions

At one point my mother came into my room to tell me that, for dinner, she had picked up a pizza at Bruno's. Since Saratoga's only local delicacy was its water, which we drank at every meal, we were free to eat a varied diet. My mom went back downstairs to put the pizza in the oven and to work until my dad came home. I kept writing. Although I had never written a newspaper article before, I had read a lot of my dad's work. I wasn't sure if I was doing justice to the story, but I knew it was a good story.

Just as my dad called out from the front hall that he was home, I was putting down the final sentences. I didn't have time to proofread, but I printed out the pages. Then I went downstairs to the kitchen, with Edmund at my side.

I held out the article for my dad to read. "What's this, Timmy?" he asked.

"Something I've been working on for quite awhile. I'd like you to read it."

"We'll have a fair trade, then, because I have something for you to read." He handed me a manila envelope. "This is the contract for the purchase of the house. Julia Green reviewed it and so did I. Everything seems to be in order, but I'd like you to look at it, before we countersign. Julia said this is the fastest transaction she's seen in twenty years of practice. Your Grandma Deena would say, 'Of course, it is. If Timmy is buying a house, he'll do it the fastest, the cheapest, and the best.'"

As my mother took the pizza out of the oven, Edmund moved close to her for a whiff.

Mom asked, "Could you two read after dinner? The pizza's hot and the salad's cold. If we wait too long, the pizza will be cold and the salad hot." I was happy to put my dull contract aside, but my dad was already hooked.

"I'll be with you in a minute, Susan." Mom and I sat down and ate slices and salad. We chatted about school and about work. We chatted about my date with Emma. We chatted about my plans for future dates with Emma.

My dad must have read the article three times. Finally, he said, "Tim, this is incredible. What a story! This isn't just a local story; this is a national story. People love this stuff. A couple of years ago, some guys claimed to have unearthed treasure in their backyard, and the public went crazy. People will love how you uncovered the clues from the attic and the basement and the garden and the desk. They'll love the false-bottomed drawer. And they'll love all the primary sources: the diary and the accounts and the recipe book and the gambling debts. It's fantastic! I'll put it on the front page of *The Saratogian* and see what wire services pick it up."

My mom said, "Do you think I could take a look?"

My dad handed her the printout, "Of course, dear. Sorry." He turned to me, "Did someone help you write this?"

"No, although I felt like Edmund's spirit was right behind me, guiding me." I stole a glance at Edmund who smiled.

My mother looked up from her reading, "That's lovely, dear. His poor, tortured soul will rest easier thanks to you."

My dad said, "Well, whatever you did to write this, keep doing it. I'm very proud of you. It's not only a great story, it's a great article. I'll need to edit it a little, but not much. Can you run upstairs and print out another copy for me?"

"Sure!" I said, jumping up out of my chair.

"What about your dinner?" my mother asked my father.

"I'll get something at the office. That pizza doesn't look very appealing." Which was true. In the interim, the cheese had congealed.

Before my dad left for the office, I finished skimming the purchase contract for the house. It was written with a lot of confusing legal terms, but I got the gist of it. When I gave my approval, my mother and father countersigned the copies, making the closing in a month official.

After Dad left, I helped Mom clean up the kitchen. Then she retired to the library to work, and Edmund and I went up to our room. I did some homework, while Edmund, exhausted by emotion, lay down on his bed.

The phone rang. My mother answered it in the library, then called up to me. I ran into the master bedroom to pick up the extension.

"Hello," I said.

"Hi, it's me," said Emma's voice. "I'm calling to tell you that I'm expecting your call in about ten seconds. Bye." She hung up.

Luckily, I still had her mother's card. I ran back down the hall, ruffled through the papers on my desk, grabbed the card, ran back to the phone and dialed. The phone rang and Emma picked up, "Hello."

"Hi," I said.

"Tim, is that you? I'm so surprised and delighted to hear from you. How are you?"

"I'm great, Emma. Really great."

"Because you're talking to me?"

"That, and because I finally figured out a real live mystery today. A murder mystery."

"That is the coolest thing I've heard in ages. Tell me about it."

So, I told her the story, including that I wrote the article. She loved hearing about the case and couldn't wait to see all my artifacts. When I asked what was happening in her life, she told me about her rehearsal and invited me to her Saturday night recital. I wasn't sure how I felt about ballet, but I was sure how I felt about Emma. I accepted.

Emma then said, "I saw Jared at lunch today. I told him about us and said that if you get hurt or harassed, I'll never talk to him again. I essentially gave him the Godfather speech about 'if some unlucky accident should befall my son Michael.' Jared wants us to remain friends, so I think he'll behave. And he's already moved on. He's dating Amanda Rodgers now."

"How quickly they forget."

"Some do, and some don't," she said. I thought of Edmund who, a hundred and twenty-five years later, was still pining for Lucy. "And some remember to call every night to check in. I have a feeling that you're going to be one of those."

"You bet I am. I'll be sure to call every night...for you."

"Aahh!" she screamed. "That's my cue to say goodnight. I still have some homework to do. Congratulations on solving the big case. I can't wait to see the article tomorrow. Remember the little people who cared about you before you were rich and famous."

"Say that part again about being rich and famous."

"I said, 'Remember the little people...'"

144

I cut her off. "Who cares about them? I want to hear about me being rich and famous."

She laughed, "I'll see you tomorrow at the bus stop."

"Where romance and diesel fumes will be in the air. Goodnight, Emma. I wish you sweet dreams."

"You, too, Tim."

* * *

My dreams were sweet, but short-lived. At five in the morning, my father woke me up to show me the hot-off-the-presses *Saratogian* with my article splashed across the front page. Luckily, Edmund slept through the noise and, to get my dad out of the room, I agreed to go downstairs to eat breakfast. While we ate at the kitchen table, Dad plied me with questions about my investigation. I was pretty sleepy, but I remembered not to mention Edmund.

My dad had decided that the murder was the perfect topic for his new novel. He would write it in first person as Charles Chatsworth, looking back over his life. In the book, Charles would eventually realize that Edmund had been murdered and that he himself was being poisoned. Charles would end the book by taking a big swig of the tainted tonic, longing for death to free him from his misery.

"It sounds really great, Dad. Is there a market for that kind of book?"

"Historical fiction is big these days. I recently read a fictitious account of Henry James's final years called *The Master*. I know James is more revered than Chatsworth, but Chatsworth's story is more intriguing."

"Then you should give it a try. What better place to write as Chatsworth than in his library, at his desk?"

"True. But I won't need his spirit to help me, because I have you. I loved your writing, Timmy. You have talent."

"Thanks, Dad."

"I want to offer you a job at the newspaper."

"As an investigative reporter?" That had always been my dream job, combining detective and writing skills.

"Not yet. We need a reporter to cover some high school sports. Would that interest you? The pay is lousy and the hours are long, but you'd get to meet lots of kids and your name would be in print."

"It sounds tempting, although I was thinking of trying out for the school play."

"Were you, now? Since when?"

Actually, since Edmund had applauded my efforts at reading aloud, but I couldn't say that. "I don't know exactly when I thought of it, but it might be worth a try."

"It's a terrific idea. You probably could do both. Might cut into your indoor basketball time, but I'm sure you could manage."

I looked at the clock on the double ovens. "I'd better get going, Dad. I've got to get to school."

"I should get going, too. This was fun. Let's do an early morning breakfast again sometime soon."

"Sure, Dad. Let's do it again next...century."

* * *

When I got to school, there were no marching bands or dancing girls or ticker-tape parades to welcome me, but Emma was waiting, which was better. She had read the article during breakfast and loved it. To say goodbye to me at homeroom, she gave me a kiss on the cheek.

Not a lot of kids had read the paper, but all my teachers had. A few of them mentioned it in class and, by the end of the day, everybody was buzzing about it. On the bus ride home, a boy from my Bio class came to sit next to me, and we did our homework together.

When I got home, Old Faithful was waiting for me at the door. We had promised each other that we would explore the attic, without fail. Before we left the kitchen, though, the telephone rang. I didn't want to answer it, but I had to. It turned out to be my dad, sounding positively giddy, because the two major wire services had picked up my story. It wouldn't be long until television news would carry it. I was pleased, but I got off the phone quickly. We had to get going.

Edmund and I went to our room and got the key. We ran up the stairs and down the hall to the locked door. I opened the door, and we ran up the steep stairs. Finally, I was in the attic in daylight.

Chapter Twenty Two

Where to begin looking? As I had remembered from my brief nocturnal visit, the attic had discarded pieces of furniture, four trunks, wooden crates with books, and some cardboard boxes. Nothing had changed. But unlike my other visit, this time I had a guide. Of course, Edmund had never dug through the trunks, crates, and boxes, but he had a pretty good idea of their contents. I asked him not to tell me too much, though, since I wanted the thrill of discovery.

In my overactive imagination, the trunks held treasure, like in my dream. I tried to open one, but found it locked. My heart sank at the idea of looking for more keys.

Edmund saved me though, pointing out, "The key is hanging down from the metal loop of the lock."

Sure enough, the key was dangling on a leather cord right in front of my eyes. I put the key in the lock and turned, then opened the trunk's lid. Inside was carefully-packed men's clothing, circa 1879, with a heavy, musty smell.

"My father's clothes," said Edmund, his voice choked with emotion.

"And the other trunks. Clothes, too?" I asked.

"Yes, one for each of us." He paused and got a grip on himself. "My clothes were moved up here shortly after I died. I suppose Hattie wanted them cleared out, but my father couldn't bear to burn them or give them to the servants, as was the custom. After my father died, his clothes came up, too. The other trunks were brought up by servants after Hattie and Albert fled. I overheard the men grumbling about carrying the trunks up, since they'd have to carry them back down when 'the missus Chatsworth sent for 'em.' Hattie must have promised the housekeeper a forwarding address. But that address clearly never came because the trunks remained here."

"The old clothing can't be very valuable, although my mother might like it for her next costume party." I was eager to move on. I walked over to the crates of books. "Edmund, would you mind if I looked through your books? Maybe there's something valuable in there."

"You're certainly welcome to look, but you won't find anything important. None of the books is a first edition or even a fine-binding. These were all my schoolbooks and, as such, were inexpensive editions."

"What about the cardboard boxes?"

"Those are of more recent vintage. Mostly clothing and playthings for young children." I lifted one flap of a box. It was filled with colorful toys from the 1920s. Nothing of value.

I noticed a smaller, lidded wooden crate mixed in with the cardboard boxes. "Is this another one of your book boxes?"

"No, I've never noticed it before. Do open it quickly." Although neither of us said anything out loud, we were both thinking of Hattie's jewels. I pulled eagerly at the lid which was held down on either side with a thin nail. I needed something to wedge between the lid and the box to get some leverage.

"I'd better run down to the kitchen and get a screwdriver," I said, resenting the break in the action more than all the stairs.

"Wait," said Edmund, "There are a few pieces of old cutlery up here. You could use a knife."

I found the cutlery box, took out a knife, and pried the lid off. There were no jewels inside--presumably Hattie had remembered to take those--but there was something special. It was the manuscript of *A Fall From Grace*, written in

Charles Chatsworth's familiar hand. I lifted out some pages and leafed through them. You could see the writer at work, changing words, crossing out phrases, inserting others.

"How wonderful!" said Edmund, getting misty-eyed again. "I feel as though my father were here with us." He sighed. "A week ago I would have thought this find very valuable, but if your mother is right, there won't be much interest in my father's work."

It was true. If this had been a long-hand manuscript of Dickens' *Great Expectations*, it would have been worth a fortune. I knew, because for my parents' twentieth anniversary, my father had asked me to search the Internet for a signed Dickens letter to give to my mother. At a reputable dealer, we had found a letter, consisting of only one line, which was a few thousand dollars. My father had decided to give my mother a Victorian bookchain necklace instead.

"Treasure is in the eye of the beholder." I said, trying to be diplomatic. "I didn't realize it at first, but this manuscript is exactly what I was hoping to find."

Edmund smiled. "Do you consider the search over or would you like to see the contents of my treasure box?"

"You have a treasure box?" Edmund nodded. "And it's up here?" He nodded again. "You've been holding out on me."

"You told me to let you have 'the thrill of discovery.'"

"Ok, now I want the thrill of discovering the contents of your treasure box. Where is it?"

Edmund pointed to the back wall near the spiral staircase. I walked over and saw a panel in the wall with a knob on it. I pulled it open. There was a storage space, built in between the outer and inner wall. A carved wooden box, about the size of a cigar box, rested there.

"Are there any other secret hiding places that I should know about?" I asked.

"Not that I am aware of," Edmund responded. "Could you please open the lid now? I haven't seen my treasures for over a century. I didn't tell Rose or Peter about the box, for fear they would take my things."

I brought the box over to the best-lit window, and Edmund and I sat down on the rough wooden floor. The box's lid was on hinges, which had rusted a bit, but with a little coaxing I managed to raise it. Edmund seemed as excited as if he were gazing at a box full of diamonds. I scanned the contents. I didn't see anything of real value, just the classic collected objects of any boy. At Edmund's request, I took out the "treasures," one at a time.

First came a white seashell.

"This seashell, called a 'chequered carpet shell,' was from an ocean holiday that I took with my family when I was about eight. My brother found it and gave it to me. Isn't it lovely?"

Then came a handkerchief with the embroidered initials CC.

"This handkerchief was my father's, embroidered by my mother. See how tiny and beautiful her stitches were. I had a dreadful illness when I was six, and the doctors feared for my life. My father gave me this hankie so that I would think of him while I lay in bed and would remember to be strong to conquer the illness."

Next came a carved shell cameo brooch, depicting three women, wearing diaphanous, flowing gowns, dancing in a circle.

"This brooch of the three Graces was from my mother. She used to wear it occasionally at her throat. My father had given it to her when he first courted her. He didn't like her to wear it, though, because it wasn't very valuable. The frame is only silver, but it had great sentimental significance to my mother. When she knew she was dying, she gave it to me and told me that, someday, I should give it to the woman I loved. She said whomever I loved would appreciate its true worth. If only I had given it to Lucy before I set sail. How I would have liked to think of her wearing the brooch."

He sighed deeply.

I tried to distract him. "The carving is really nice. And the subject matter is great. Anyone who likes dancing would like this brooch."

"Your Emma is a dancer, isn't she?"

"I'm not sure we can call her mine yet, but, yes, she is a dancer."

"I should like you to give her the brooch."

"Edmund, that's way too generous. You need the brooch. We can leave it out someplace where you can look at it whenever you want."

"No, Tim, the brooch is meant to be worn. And it needs to be worn by a person who will appreciate it. Emma sounds like that kind of person. Tell her you found my treasure box and that you suspect that it was my mother's and, therefore, important to me. I'm sure she'll like it."

"Thanks, Edmund, I'm sure she will. She has a big recital on Saturday. I was going to I buy her some flowers, but I'll give her this instead."

Edmund said, smiling, "And don't eat any garlic or onions before you give it to her. Girls like to show their appreciation for nice gifts."

"Got it," I said.

We turned back to the treasure box. There was a pressed red rose from his mother which was remarkably well-preserved, his first report card from Eton with impressive marks, and a lock of dark brown hair.

"Lucy allowed me to cut this off at our last meeting...." He couldn't say anything more for a while.

I put everything back in the treasure box except the brooch. "Would you like me to put the box back or bring it downstairs?"

"Let's bring the treasure box and the manuscript down to our room. That way, I can look at them any time you're around."

I gathered our booty and headed carefully downstairs. When we got to the third floor landing, I could hear the phone ringing. I raced down the next flight and flew into my parents' room, grabbing the receiver. It was my dad calling.

"Tim, where have you been all afternoon? I've called a dozen times."

"Sorry, Dad, I didn't hear the phone ring." I decided I might as well tell him where I'd been. I didn't need to keep it a secret anymore. "I was exploring the attic."

"More detective work, huh?"

"Sort of. I found something really cool. I found the original manuscript of Charles Chatsworth's last book."

"Wow! I can use it to help me with my new book. It will give me a sense of Chatsworth's methodology as a writer."

"Great. So, why were you calling?"

"Oh, I was calling to say that a bunch of news and morning programs have asked for interviews. The morning programs invited you to come to New York, but I said you couldn't miss school. *Wake Up, America* has offered to send a crew to the house. That is, if you're interested."

"They want to talk to me? Shouldn't they talk to you?"

"You're the guy who did all the investigating, solved the mystery, and wrote the article. They have no interest in me."

"Do you think I should do it? I didn't solve the mystery to get attention, and I'll probably freeze-up on camera."

"I'm sure you would be great, but the decision is yours."

It occurred to me that Edmund would be delighted to have a wide audience hear his story. "Oh, what the heck, you only live once. Sure, I'll go on television and make a fool of myself."

"Grandma Deena will be thrilled to see you with 'that lovely Diane Summers.' Ok, I'd better call these people back. They've been breathing down my neck all afternoon."

When I hung up, I explained to Edmund that I and the house would be on televisions--lots of little boxes all over the country--the next day.

Chapter Twenty Three

The rest of the day passed in a blur. I had to finish my homework, eat dinner, and talk to each set of grandparents. The Cohens said they hoped I'd have fun and were sure I'd do well, the Rosses were sure I would either be a huge success or a dismal failure, and they all told me that their entire housing center would be watching. I remembered to call Emma who was thrilled that I would be on television, but disappointed that she'd have to watch it on tape after school. My mom helped me pick out clothes for the interview. She insisted that I model each outfit, which was a pain, but turned out to be necessary because not everything fit. We finally agreed on khakis, a light blue button-down shirt, and my navy sweater. By eight o'clock I was exhausted, having been up since five in the morning. I had to get up at five-thirty the next morning for hair and makeup, so I conceded defeat and went to bed.

It felt like I had just shut my eyes when my alarm clock buzzed. Edmund was already awake, sitting on his bed, watching me. I was about to say that I had slept like a dead man, but stopped myself from being rude. I crawled out of bed and threw myself into the shower.

The television crew showed up while I was getting dressed. They were all lively and cheerful, as if it were two in the afternoon. When I went downstairs, with Edmund in tow, I was nabbed by a pleasant, ultra-thin woman who sat me at the kitchen table to work on me. Although I protested vehemently, she powdered my face. I felt quietly vindicated that she, a professional, had trouble with my hair.

When my makeup was finished, another young woman, this one with a clipboard and pen, got custody of me. She asked me questions about school and home and my investigation. She smiled a lot and nodded encouragingly as she made notes. Edmund stood over her shoulder reading the notes and told me when she had gotten something wrong. I did a lot of clarifying, without her asking, and by the end she declared me clairvoyant.

I had been worried that the morning would drag since I wasn't scheduled to be on until 8:17. Before I knew it, though, I was being called into the living room and seated on the sofa. The living room had been transformed with bright lights, cameras, and a monitor on which I could watch Diane Summers. At about 8:05, during a commercial break, Diane Summers talked to me over the monitor to say that she really loved my story and that I should just relax and be myself. I was waiting for her to tell me to stay away from garlic and onions. She advised me to answer questions promptly to maintain the flow of the conversation.

The monitor stayed on to show the two segments before my turn. Behind the camera crew stood my parents and Mr. Henry, who we had invited over. My dad gave me a thumbs-up. Edmund came over to sit with me on the sofa. He whispered, although no one else could have heard him, " Good luck, Tim. You're going to be more entertaining than Charles Dickens."

And then I heard Diane Summers saying, "Remember the story of the Sleeping Beauty who slept for 100 years, waiting for her handsome prince to awaken her with a kiss? Well, this morning we have a story about a real live mystery that slept for over a hundred years, waiting to be solved by just the right reporter."

She gave the broad outlines of my investigation, noting that no one had ever realized there was a mystery, and then asked me questions. They were exactly the kind of questions adults ask kids, like "Were you excited when you found the diary?" (duh) and "How do you think this discovery will change your life?" (not very much).

Only two questions really stood out for me. First, she asked me, "Has your detective work been inspired by great TV detective shows like *Murder From Her Pen* and *Courts and Police*?" As instructed, I answered quickly. "Not really. You see, we don't own a television set."

What a change in Diane Summers' face! It had been, well, a summer's day, and now it changed to stormy weather. Not only had I told about five million viewers that we thought little of television, but I had put down two of the network's top programs. I quickly added that I read a lot of detective novels, but that didn't make things any better.

The other unexpected question was, "There have been reports that Chatsworth Mansion is haunted. Have you seen any ghosts lately?"

I was tempted to say, "Yes, there's one sitting on the sofa next to me," but I didn't. I said, "I really can't tell you if there are ghosts," which was true, "but I can tell you that there's a special spirit to this house. My mom, dad, and I all feel it, and we are very fortunate to be living here."

Diane Summers wrapped up her report about good triumphing over evil, even though sometimes is takes a long time. Then it was over. When I stood up, I discovered that my knees were shaky. My mom thought it was because I hadn't eaten breakfast so, while the camera crew dismantled, my parents, Mr. Henry, and I went into the kitchen to eat. Then my dad announced that my fifteen minutes of fame were over, and he was driving me to school.

When I arrived at school, I went directly to the principal's office to get a late pass. The secretary patted her hair as I handed her the note explaining my tardiness. She said that Principal Cooper wanted to see me, and my full stomach turned over. Who knew that the school took attendance so seriously?

But I had it all wrong. Principal Cooper didn't want to lecture me on punctuality, he wanted to congratulate me. It turns out that Emma had gone to school early and marched into his office to inform him that one of his students was going to be on national TV. Although not usually a decisive man, Principal Cooper had ordered a large TV to be set up in the auditorium and, over the loudspeakers, had called the entire school to an assembly. Every person in Saratoga High, from the teachers to the students to the secretaries to the custodians, had watched my interview. Principal Cooper had been delighted by my appropriate noises about liking my new school, which he felt reflected well on him.

He shook my hand and said, "This is a proud day for Saratoga Springs, and a proud day for Saratoga Springs High." Then he sent me off to class.

The halls were empty, which was a relief. I didn't want to have to face my schoolmates any sooner than necessary. I wasn't sure how they'd react to the media attention. Would they be excited or jealous? Supportive or mocking?

As I tried to quietly slip into my English class, I got my answer. My fellow students erupted in applause and whistles. Miss McMahon had a tough time calming them down and finally gave up on trying to discuss *The Great Gatsby* and, instead, allowed the kids to ask me questions about the interview and the murder mystery.

I was glad it was Friday, so the furor could die down over the weekend. I could scarcely walk through the hallways to my classes. Everyone had a question or comment to make, all of them positive. It turns out that being on TV is a big deal. Even kids who formerly had tormented me, came up to say things like, "Good job, Bite Size," and "Way to go, Short Stuff." On the bus, kids fought to sit next to me, and had to work out a rotation based on the order of their bus stops.

When I got home, Edmund was waiting. We greeted each other warmly, and I suggested that I make a snack—maybe hot chocolate and warmed chocolate chip cookies—for him to smell and me to eat. I observed that this was the first time all week that we weren't rushing to explore something.

"Actually, Tim, I wanted to suggest one more excursion."

"Where to?"

"Remember you thought you could take me out in your backpack? Well, I'd like to go to visit my father's grave."

I had heard that Chatsworth's tombstone was nice on my very first day in Saratoga, when I'd asked Mr. Henry for directions, but I had never gone to see it.

"Have bike, will travel," I said.

"You wouldn't mind too much?"

"Not at all." I was actually a little nervous about taking Edmund to the cemetery. There was a good chance that his own tombstone would be right near his father's and that could prove unsettling. Still, I felt an obligation to grant him this request.

"I have a special favor to ask of you while we're there," said Edmund.

"What's that?"

"I'd like you to bury my treasure box near my tombstone," he said.

"Edmund, I don't understand. You've been without your keepsakes for so long and now that you have them, you're getting rid of them."

"I know it seems a bit odd to you, but it feels right to me. If I keep the treasures where I can see them, someone might throw them out or give them away. If I keep them safe in the attic cupboard, I won't get to see them. But if I bury them, they'll always be near a part of me."

"Well, they're your treasures, so it's your decision."

"Then let's go to the cemetery before it gets too dark or windy."

* * *

158

When we arrived at the cemetery, we passed an elderly woman talking out loud to a tombstone as if it were her neighbor. I guess she needed answers to some important questions.

I knew exactly where to go, having looked up the information in Mr. Henry's Saratoga book. I was carrying my oversized backpack over my right arm. It weighed almost nothing. I had left the top part of the zipper undone so I could frequently check on Edmund, who had folded himself in like a contortionist. The arrangement didn't look very comfortable, but he assured me it was fine.

You couldn't miss the Chatsworth monument. It had a huge, stone pedestal about four feet high and, on top, a full body statue of Charles, holding a book in his left hand against his chest and a quill pen in his right hand. Hattie, perhaps in hopes of solidifying her own social standing, had spared no expense memorializing her famous husband. Edmund peeked his head out through the zippered opening and seemed pleased.

Finding where Edmund was buried proved more difficult. I was looking for a headstone, but eventually discovered that all Edmund got was a small, rectangular stone marker in the ground next to his father's massive memorial. It was particularly hard to find because leaves were covering most of it. I cleared them away and checked to make sure no one was around before I spoke. Then I showed the marker to Edmund.

"I hope you're not disappointed," I said.

"No, I'm just glad that I'm right next to my father. I wasn't expecting much, really. Not after the diary entry."

"Do you still want me to bury your treasure box?" I had brought along my all-purpose digging spoon, the one I had used in the herb garden.

"Yes, I do," said Edmund. He ducked back in.

I had to dig for awhile to make a hole big enough and deep enough for the box. My thoughts kept drifting to poor

Charles Chatsworth, who had come to this spot to bury his beloved son, feeling guilty for his boy's death and helpless to secure a proper funeral.

Out of the front pouch of the backpack, I removed the box and placed it in the hole. I said, "Edmund, I'm going to cover the box now. Would you mind if I said a few words?"

"Is it safe for you to be seen talking to yourself?"

"While I was digging, I realized it doesn't matter. People talk to themselves or, I suppose, their loved ones, all the time in cemeteries. I think it's totally safe."

"Then I'd like it very much."

I paused a moment to collect my thoughts as I pushed loose dirt over the box. Then I said, "Here lies Edmund Chatsworth. He was cheated of his life by a horrible fiend, the cruel Albert who put the demands of his purse above the value of Edmund's life. Edmund has endured a long time without peace, but now at least he has understanding. He always knew that he had been murdered, but he didn't know why or by whom. I hope this new understanding will make his existence more tolerable."

I heard Edmund quietly crying, but I couldn't stop. There were things I wanted to say. "Edmund died way too young, but his death shouldn't define his life. He was intelligent, educated, handsome, kind, and clever. He was beloved by his father, his mother, his brother, and his cousin Lucy. He was a good person and a good friend. I should know, because he is my friend...my best friend."

I realized Edmund's crying was growing fainter. I looked over at him and, it was the weirdest thing, but he seemed to be growing fainter, too.

"Edmund, what's happening?"

"I don't know, Tim," he answered in a voice that was barely audible.

"Are you blowing away? I can zip up the back-pack."

"No, I'm not blowing away."

I had to really strain to hear him.

"Are you in any pain?" I asked, my voice rising with anxiety.

"On the contrary, I feel so warm and happy."

"Do you think you're going to a better place?"

I couldn't see him anymore, but I thought I heard a whisper in the air say, "Bingo."

I grabbed hold of the backpack, opened the zipper wider, and looked inside. Then I turned the backpack inside-out and shook it. I even checked the small front pouch. The backpack was empty. Edmund was gone.

I began to cry, first with tears that ran down my cheeks, then with sobs that shook my whole body. I told myself I was crying because I was happy for Edmund, which was partially true, but mostly I was crying because I was sad for me. Although Edmund hadn't been part of my life for long, now that he was gone, I felt completely and utterly alone.

I cried for a long time. When I realized that my tears were evidence of Edmund's influence, I cried even more. Some people walked by, staring, but no one said anything. In a cemetery, seeing someone crying is even more commonplace than seeing someone talking to himself.

The sun was starting to set, and it was getting cold. I hadn't left a note for my mom and, if she had gotten home, she would be worried. I didn't want to leave the cemetery, but I had to. I choked out a last "goodbye" in case Edmund could hear me.

Chapter Twenty Four

Edmund's disappearance felt like the end of the story, but it was only the end of a chapter. Life goes on. I biked home to find both parents waiting for me, bubbling over with excitement from the morning interview. The returns were in, and everyone in Saratoga--from my dad's colleagues on the newspaper to my mom's colleagues at the college to the cashier at Putnam Market--was thrilled.

My parents were so euphoric, in fact, that they were oblivious to my somber mood. It wasn't until my mom took a vegetable lasagna out the oven and served it that she noticed something was amiss. Usually, the lasagna was a big hit with me, but instead of digging in, I sat and inhaled its aromatic steam.

"Timmy, are you all right?" she asked.

"Sure, Mom, I'm fine. Just a little tired I guess."

My dad said, "Of course, you're tired. You've gotten up early two days in a row and had big days, to boot. Luckily, tomorrow's Saturday, and you can sleep as late as you want."

"Sleep sounds like a good idea. I'm not very hungry. Do you mind if I go up to my room now?"

My dad said, "No problem," but my mom came over to put her lips to my forehead, checking for a fever, before she'd let me go.

I dragged myself up the stairs and went to our room. Make that my room. It seemed awfully empty without Edmund on the butterfly chair or on the extra bed. I was exhausted and, fortunately, I didn't have to call Emma who had a dress rehearsal.

I got ready for bed, climbed in, and turned out the light. I tried to think how Edmund would want me to feel about his disappearance. Because he had told me about Lucy, I knew that he would want me to be--how had he put it?--touched, but not ruined. It was sad to lose a friend, but it was a bittersweet sadness. Thanks to Edmund, my life had become much better and, while I would miss him, I would think of him often. How could I not? There were so many reminders of him everywhere, including his wonderful lighthouse room where I lay in bed.

I closed my eyes and slept.

* * *

In my television interview I had said, with absolute certainty, that uncovering the mystery wouldn't change my life. It turns out, I was absolutely wrong.

On Saturday, as scheduled, I went to see Emma dance in her recital. She was wonderful. I clapped so hard for her solo piece that my hands hurt. After the recital, I met her backstage and presented her with a wrapped box. She opened it and, upon seeing the brooch, threw her arms around me. If she had had any doubts about me, the brooch made them disappear. I might be just a little fish, but she wouldn't throw me back.

A month later, my family closed on the house. As soon as we owned it, we applied to the National Registry for permission to paint. My dad played up the house's newfound media attention and got the bureaucrats to respond quickly. Not surprisingly, they said yes. Surprisingly, Mr. Henry organized a group of neighbors to have the equivalent of a barn-raising, only this was a house-painting. Since they were all sick of the eyesore, they were eager to pitch in. Once the weather was temperate, which in Saratoga meant the end of May, the house was restored to its original light brown. It looked very handsome and not at all spooky.

During the long winter, my mom made her way through all fourteen of the Chatsworth novels. Then she sat down and, in a week's time, wrote a paper on "The Evolution of Style and Content in the Works of Charles Chatsworth." She sent off the paper to a top literary journal, not expecting much, but confident that her work was unusual and original. Within two weeks, the paper was accepted.

My dad was equally busy that winter. While my mom sat in the library and read, he sat in the library and wrote. By spring, he had finished his historical novel about Chatsworth and, through one of Mom's Skidmore friends, got it read by an agent in New York City. The agent loved it and swore she would get it published, which she did. The book came out a year later and had the success of strong reviews and solid sales.

A movie studio that specializes in highbrow costume dramas bought the rights to the book and begged to film the movie in our house. They agreed to pay a modest sum to use the house and, more importantly, agreed to permanently furnish the main rooms in period style. Mr. Henry clinched the deal by inviting us to live with him for the six weeks of filming. After the film crews left, the inside of the house was as restored to its former glory as the outside.

Because Edmund had charged me with rehabilitating his father's literary reputation, I was thrilled that my dad's book and movie sparked an interest in Chatsworth's work among the general public which dovetailed nicely with the interest my mom's work sparked in literary circles. One publisher decided to come out with new editions of three of Chatsworth's works. The publisher consulted with my mother on the selection, and hired her to write the forewords. As Chatsworth's star rose, so did my mom's. She was the world's foremost Chatsworth authority. We didn't point out that she was the only Chatsworth authority. Skidmore, afraid of losing my mom to a bigger school, offered her a full professorship. She happily accepted.

Since Chatsworth was a British author, the story of the murder was big news in England. Quite a few newspapers and magazines called to interview me. I mentioned in one that I had discovered the manuscript of Chatsworth's last novel. The news must have crossed the desk of the Director of the British Library because one day I received a call from him, saying that it was in his country's national interest to purchase the manuscript.

I had visited the British Library with my parents and seen the permanent exhibit that includes works by authors such as Chaucer, Shakespeare, Bronte, Austen, and Joyce. I couldn't think of a better place for the Chatsworth manuscript to land, but I played hardball. My terms were not about payment, but about use. I told the Director that I would sell the manuscript at a "fair price," to be set by the Library, if the Library would sign an agreement to exhibit the manuscript next to their Dickens display. The Library accepted my conditions, paying me a princely sum from private donations, and Chatsworth got to reside in the pantheon of authors, just as Edmund had wanted.

To have a Chatsworth exhibit closer to home, I took a chunk of the British Library money and donated it to the Saratoga Springs Visitor Center, conveniently located at the beginning of Broadway, near the Adelphi Hotel. The Center put together a terrific permanent display about Chatsworth that included items on loan from my family such as authentic Victorian clothing, Edmund's spectacles, Chatsworth's diary and household accounts, the garden tags, the glass jar labeled "wormwood," the stillroom recipe book, Albert's horse racing receipts, an enlarged photograph of the broken railing, and Albert's date book.

Albert's date book was a more recent find. When the curator for the Center had Albert's dress coat cleaned for the exhibit, a small black date book was discovered in the breast pocket. The date book covered a two year period, including the date of Edmund's death. For that day, Albert had written, in script that matched the horse-racing debts:

Dining with Sybil

Meeting with Edmund

Dancing with Mabel at Fair

Although I hadn't needed any more proof of Albert's guilt, the entry felt like the proverbial last nail in the coffin. Since Edmund and Albert had had nothing to do with each other, their "meeting" that must have been unilaterally arranged. I wished I could tell Edmund of the new discovery.

There were a lot of things I wished I could tell Edmund. I missed him keenly for a long time. Not having him at home gave me incentive to stay out. I worked hard as a sports reporter for *The Saratogian*, and I got the lead in the school play, *Blithe Spirit*, which, ironically, is about a writer who is visited by the ghost of his dead first wife. My schedule was packed, which was good because Emma was busy with ballet. She and I talked every night and saw each other whenever we could. We were in great demand among our peers, but we made sure to find time to be alone. We made each other laugh, we made each other think, and we made each other happy.

The crowd at Saratoga High School didn't miraculously transform, but we found some friends. I even came to like Jared who, as Emma had said, was sweet and loyal, albeit boring. His strongest draw was his long-term girlfriend, Amanda Rodgers. In the spring, Jared planned a big party to which Emma and I were invited. A couple of days before the event, Stephanie cornered me in the hall to ask if I could get her an invitation since I "was such a good friend of Jared's." I hadn't even known that she had been excluded, but I assume Jared had done it on my behalf. Stephanie must have made a major withdrawal from the self-esteem bank to ask me for a favor, so I decided to be, as my dad would say, generous and gracious. I got her invited to the party. You have to do those sorts of things when you're a "big" man on campus, which I mean figuratively, not literally.

I did grow some that year, which is why my clothes didn't fit on the night before my interview, but I didn't get the substantial growth spurt I had wanted. Still, nobody seemed to mind my lack of height, including Emma, so I stopped worrying.

The vision that I had upon first hearing about Chatsworth Mansion actually came true: people stopped by to ask for tours. Some people came because they were interested in Chatsworth, others because the house itself had become a celebrity. We were always happy to drop what we were doing to show people around. We figured that the house had stood empty for so long that it needed to catch-up in feeling occupied and admired.

My father's prediction that the house would be a *good* investment was wrong; it was a *great* investment. Periodically, realtors would call to say they had a client who was dying to buy Chatsworth Mansion. We just had to name the price. One realtor who was particularly pushy on the point was the indomitable Ellen Stilton. She had a client hell-bent on owning the place, and Mrs. Stilton, knowing what we had paid for it, had assured her client that she would "make the deal happen." Because the offer was many times what we had paid for the house, probably many times its true value, Mrs. Stilton was confident she would triumph. After days of harassing phone calls in which she tried to persuade, cajole, sweet-talk, and bully us into a deal, my father told Mrs. Stilton that she was forbidden to ever call again. He decided that she was one Saratogian he affirmatively wanted to alienate.

Although we took some small satisfaction in disappointing Mrs. Stilton, the truth was we wouldn't sell to anybody. We weren't interested. The house was no longer an investment, it was a home. I knew that, as I grew up and went to college and took jobs, I would probably have to live in different cities, but I also knew that I would never sell Chatsworth Mansion. Saratoga may have reached its heyday in the Victorian era, but it was still a wonderful town. And the house, even without Edmund, continued to have a special spirit. Maybe we would have generated that spirit elsewhere on our own, but we weren't interested in trying. Chatsworth would remain my permanent residence for the rest of my life, and I would never again have to start a personal account with "It was moving day."

A Note From the Author

Near the end of the book, Tim mentions London's British Library, which I consider a must-see attraction for lovers of great literature. If you've ever been there, I'm sure you're nodding your head in agreement. If you've never been there, plan to go sometime in your life and, in the interim, visit the website at http://www.bl.uk/onlinegallery/homepage.html

In the British Library's collection, you won't find any works by Charles Chatsworth (he's just a fictitious character), but you will find lots of other wonderful things. I can never decide whether I'm more excited about the original "Alice's Adventures in Wonderland," handwritten and illustrated by Lewis Carroll, or "The History of England," handwritten and illustrated by a young Jane Austen. Fortunately, I don't have to decide and can page through both of them whenever I feel like it. And now, so can you.